A Wild Winter Swan

ALSO BY GREGORY MAGUIRE

Fiction

Hiddensee

After Alice

The Next Queen of Heaven

Lost

Mirror Mirror

Confessions of an Ugly Stepsister

The Wicked Years

Wicked

Son of a Witch

A Lion Among Men

Out of Oz

For Younger Readers

Matchless

Egg & Spoon

What-the-Dickens

Missing Sisters

The Good Liar

Leaping Beauty

Nonfiction

Making Mischief: A Maurice Sendak Appreciation

A Wild Winter Swan

A Novel

Gregory Maguire

HARPER LARGE PRINT
An Imprint of HarperCollins*Publishers*

The adaptation from the Latin of the Aquitanian lyric is by Anne Azéma and is used with her permission.

FIRST HARPER LARGE PRINT EDITION

ISBN: 978-0-06-302889-0

Library of Congress Cataloging-in-Publication Data is available upon request.

20 21 22 23 24 LSC 10 9 8 7 6 5 4 3 2 1

for my brothers and sisters

John, Rachel, Michael, Matthew, Annie, and Joe

Clangam filii,
ploratione une alitis cigne,
qui transfretavit equora.
O quam amara lamentabatur,
Arida se dereliquisse florigera
Et petisse alta maria aiens:
Infelix sum avicula
heu mihi
quid agam misera.
Pennis solute inniti lucida
Non potero hic in stilla.
Undis quatior,
Procellis hic intense alidor exulata.

—Anonymous,
Carolingian-Aquitanian origin,
c. A.D. 850

Hear me, children,
sing the lamentation of the Swan
that flew out over the water.

Oh how he grieved,
for he had given up the firm land
for the high seas.
This was his bitter cry:
"I am an unlucky bird.
Alas,
how shall I endure such misery?
My wings will not support me,
the waves batter me,
the winds dash me in my exile."

—TRANSLATION BY ANNE AZÉMA,
BOSTON CAMERATA

There's a story—the sixth brother. Give him something to do. The boy with a wing. You know the one I mean?

—P. L. TRAVERS,
AUTHOR OF *MARY POPPINS*,
IN CONVERSATION WITH THE AUTHOR,
OCTOBER 1995

1

Knuckles of hail rapped against Laura's window with a musical jumpiness. Hardly tidings of comfort and joy, comfort and joy, though, when the room was an icebox. Coming downstairs to get warm, Laura trailed her hand on the greens wound round the banister. This raised a note of balsam in the air. But she knew better than to trust the false hope of the holidays.

Every green garland ends up in the ash can.

She paused, in a silence rich and pertinent to herself if to no one else, and told herself into the moment. Not a silent narration spoken in her mind, but a story as it felt, something more or less like this:

In the city of New York once stood a house on Van Pruyn Place. It was owned by a fierce old Italian importer known as Ovid Ciardi, of Ciardi's Fine Foods and Delicacies. His stout hobbley wife lived there, too, griping the whole livelong day. Their granddaughter had come to live with them, nobody remembered why. One day she walked down the shiny fancy stairs to find two workers in the front hall. Fellows who had come out on a Saturday, no less, to repair the grouting of the stone windowsills on the top floor. But they were puttering around here instead. One was climbing a stepladder that had been set up in a circle of plaster dust and fallen fragments of ceiling. They didn't notice the girl. She was fifteen and had long brown hair, very straight. She wished her eyes were mossy green but they were Italian brown, espresso brown. The workers didn't notice her eyes or her. They were staring at something else.

That was as far as she could go. She didn't know what happened next because it hadn't happened yet. "What are you doing?"

From a hole in the plaster ceiling John Greenglass withdrew a baby—a baby something. An owl? It was still alive. "This *is* an item," said John. He backed down the stepladder, cupping with both hands the clot of fussing feather. His helper, Sam, steadied him. Laura watched from the landing.

"Come lookit, such a surprise," said Sam, gesturing.

Laura was not meant to be downstairs while the workers were there. But so much of the ordinary was overturned now. She approached as John opened his hands. Beneath the grit and plaster dust, the creature was nearly white all over. It shivered and half-flexed its wings. Maybe shocked, and also a bit of *what's-it-to-you?*

"Little scamp's scared witless," said Sam.

"How did it get in our ceiling?" asked Laura.

John shrugged. "The coping on the roof was a mess. Mortar joints washed out. That's where the water got in. But I don't know how a baby owl could wriggle inside and make its way down three flights behind the walls and across this ceiling."

"Well," said Sam affably, "maybe a rat caught it and dragged it inside."

"No rats," said Laura. Rats didn't fit into a Christmas story, even in a bitter season.

"You're too old to be blind to rats in the city, Miz Laura." Sam made cooing sounds at the small owl, who didn't reply. "What're you, fourteen?"

"Fifteen."

John shook his head. "Fifteen, Miss Laura, too grown-up to shiver at real life." Mocking her grandfather's accent, John pronounced Laura's name broadly, in three syllables: *Laow—OO—rah.* Like the bulb horn of an old-timey Model T.

"It's scared to death. Let it go," she said.

John shrugged. "You're the boss."

Sam was more tender than John. "Give it here, John. I can take it in my lunch box and bring it to the park when it's ready. Some other birds will raise it up."

"A dog will eat her, or a cat," Laura protested.

The door under the back stairs, which led to the kitchen below, swung open. Out lurched Mary Bernice, alerted by the fuss. "You's not to be loitering in the hall with no contractors," said the cook. "Laura Ciardi, you get upstairs as you're told to do. No consorting. Not on my watch."

"You're not in charge of me," said Laura. Hardly a withering retort, but she was better with sentences in her head than in her mouth.

"I'm keeping you safe from your elders lest they get word of such shenanigans." Like some kind of stage nanny, the cook flapped her apron at Laura.

"She doing nobody harm, Laura a good girl," said

Sam. "Lookee, my baby owl. It gots eyes like little black punch holes."

"For sure, if a bird comes in the house, a death comes next," replied Mary Bernice. "Get it out for once and for all. Laura, your grandda will be home any moment. Trouble twice over and never mind apologies. *Will* you get back upstairs while there's young fellows working on the premises. Go now as I'm telling you, go."

The white bird twisted its head on its neck and glared across the room to where Laura stood on the stairs.

The little owl baby looked at the orphan girl as if wanting to give her a message. But then the handsome workman closed his hand again and dropped the owl into his companion's lunch box. The lid fell shut softly, and softly did the clasps clasp. The little owl in darkness. Like a tomb.

"She'll suffocate in there," said Laura.

"It's a she? Okay then. I'll see she gets some air and something to eat," said Sam. Laura didn't know his last name. He was on his way to being dark-skinned and had a soft, sing-along voice. "If she can fly, why, I'll let her fly away."

"How did you even know there was a baby owl in the ceiling?" asked Laura.

John said, "We were tracking the leak from the ledge outside your window, up top of the house. It runs down the wall of the master bedroom below you. Stained your grandparents' room, then skipped the parlor below that. Must've followed an internal channel, and so it emerges here. Water does that." Hence, Laura supposed, the torn and crumbled plaster and the glimpse of lathes. "Reached in to see how much rot we'd have to pull down, and what do we find but this little bundle. Surprises in New York City every day of the year, I always say."

"Your grandfather, he won't be happy to see this surprise, the week before Christmas," said Sam.

"O come all ye faithful," sang John, "joyful and triumphant." Then, speaking, "I always wondered why not, O come all ye doubtful, lazybones and losers."

"They're invited too," said Mary Bernice, "but they have to stand in back because there's an unruly number of them. Hoo, listen up and buckle your britches, lads, the mister's on the stoop. Laura, shoo!"

Laura flew up the stairs, reaching the second floor just as the key turned in the front door and her grandfather came in, stomping snow off his overshoes. At the sight of the mess in the front hall, a sound of under-his-breath cursing in Italian.

Across the landing Laura tiptoed. She bypassed the office and the parlor doors, and pivoted to the back staircase, which went down to the kitchen and upstairs too. She rose to the floor above, skirting the door to her grandparents' room, and up once more, till she reached the top of the house.

The governess's room, unused since Laura was twelve, was full of junk removed from the box room. Opposite the top of the stairs, across the landing, Laura's little bathroom was squeezed in alongside the bricks of the chimney stack. In the front of the house, two pinched rooms. The box room stood haunted and echoey on the right-hand side, empty but for some tools and buckets and work gloves on the floor. On the left, Laura's bedroom. Its single window, set in a slanting ceiling inside the mansard roof of the top flight, was filled with white wings.

She saw wings.

No, not wings. Shadows of snowflakes, big fat snowflakes falling outside in the icy December dusk.

2

Laura threw herself on her bed. She lay in velvet shadow. She took in how things looked in the slop of her own life. The hall light, slanting through her doorway, picked out the grey-sheeted linoleum tacked in place with brass strips, the faded flowery wallpaper. Here and there the archaic lilacs were browned with waterstains from other winter leaks.

She could hear the rhythm of Nonno's interview with John and Sam. Subdued and civil tones, until the front door opened again and Nonna came in. Laura's grandmother had never sung on the stage and her voice could hardly be called musical, but she clinched her entrance every time like a pro.

Whose story is it now? Whoever talks the loudest when they walk through the door, do they own it?

Right on schedule, the orchestrated hysterics of Laura's grandmother. That baby owl, trapped in a lunch box, probably scared to death from the drama. Behind the door to the kitchen steps Mary Bernice was listening, too, Laura would bet on it.

Isabella Bentivengo Ciardi would be clutching the two ends of the fox fur around her neck as she harangued the men who had perpetrated this inconvenience, it amounted to a catastrophe, a disaster, *Madonna mia!* That last was not a curse, but a prayer. Mother of God, what you ask of me now, eh? prayed Nonna Ciardi. A dinner was to happen here this week, did none of them understand this?

Laura got every syllable. Nonna Ciardi didn't need mechanical assistance when she was ready to broadcast the state of her nervous disposition. Nonno said his wife could be heard nightly from Hell's Kitchen to Astoria, and on clear nights as far as Randalls Island.

"But Vito, Vito, we have family coming on Christmas Eve, my elevated sister, her superior husband. And our house looking now like what, like what, I ask you? Like a goat shed on a back road in Calabria! What it says to them? I ask you, Vito!" The more upset she got, the closer she came to losing the Rules of Better Speech that she picked up at the Ladies' Auxiliary seminars at church on Tuesdays.

Nonno's voice was quiet but firm. He preferred to be called Ovid, or Signore Ciardi. Vito was too old country, Vito was too Esquilino, too down-and-out-in-Mussolini's-Rome. *Ovid* was *Vito* turned backward, sort of, and the first vowel softened. To his wife he now became prophetic. The ceiling would be repaired. The guests would be delighted by this lovely house in Van Pruyn Place. They need not know how it had come into Vito's possession. They need not hear that the ceiling had just collapsed. It would look rich as Rockefeller's.

"Jenny and her man will smell the raw paint, Vito, they will smell desperation!"

"And if loose stone from top of house fall on their heads as they stand at front door, Bella? That would be better to happen? *Buon Natale, riposa in pace?*"

Laura could not hear any more of what Nonno Ciardi was saying to calm down his wife, but her voice dropped, *pianissimo,* until what carried up three flights of steps was only the urgency of her syllables.

Laura watched the snow make feathers upon her wall. The snow had a glow of its own. The afternoon darkened. Downstairs, doors opened and closed emphatically.

The girl thought: Doors have a language, too. They talk to each other.

The workers were returning materials to John Greenglass's rusty old blue truck, probably. Even if Laura had stood and craned, she wouldn't have been able to see it at the curb. The street too narrow, the house too high.

From below, Mary Bernice hissing. Her voice like the rasp of a match on sandpaper. (She smoked every night after washing up the dinner dishes.) "You're wanted in the parlor, Laura. Your granny needs to speak to you."

Laura waited on her bedspread until Mary Bernice called again, just to hear the increased impatience in the cook's voice. Then Laura darted down two flights, slowing to a more ladylike pace as she approached the parlor. The cook was lurking with a beady expression. "Bring in this tea for me, will you? And Laura—I'm going to church tonight. You want to come with me?"

"You think I'm in need of grace, too?" said Laura's words, but her tone said *Nope*.

"Laura," cooed Nonna without looking up. She was

flipping through the mail. Her ankles were crossed upon the new wall-to-wall, which still smelled of glue and resin. Laura examined her grandmother.

The old woman was worn out. Her hands trembled as she tore open the bill from the Consolidated Edison Company. Her lips pursed in worry. Who knew what troubles rested upon those stooped shoulders?

"Don't stand there gaping like a chimpanzee. Close the door. There's a draft with all that coming and going. My tea, please, and then sit down. I haven't got all night," said Nonna.

Actually the old grandmother was something of a bitch.

No, that was too intense, but Laura couldn't rethink it now. She crossed the room, leaving footprints in the plush pile of the rug that Mary Bernice would eradicate tomorrow with the carpet sweeper.

"So much to try to manage at this time of year," said Nonna. Laura waited. Nonna's rhetorical practice was to review her schedule of troubles aloud before alighting on the one appropriate to her audience. "My sister

Geneva and her mighty husband, Mr. Corm Kennedy, are coming for Christmas Eve. She's your great-aunt. I've told you this." Nonna had recovered her artificial upper-class diction, sort of.

"You sure have. Is Mr. Corm Kennedy related to our president?" asked Laura.

"I doubt President John Fitzgerald Kennedy would even know. He has had other things on his mind, what with all this Cuba annoyance. His is a large Irish family with a thousand cousins. But you must not ask Mr. Corm Kennedy about *his* relations. I'm told that's rude."

"Mary Bernice could ask him. She's from Ireland."

"Don't interrupt, Laura. And don't be nosy. Listen to me. Since Mr. Corm Kennedy is a new member of our family and my glamorous sister is trying to show him off, I want us to appear the equal to him. Good with the manners, perfect with the food. Sure in our feeting. Footing. Unashamed, Laura, because we have nothing to be ashamed *about*. Do you understand?"

"You've mentioned this before, Nonna. Every night for two weeks."

Nonna sighed. "Hand me my wrap from the pouffe, please Laura, I can't shake the chill. A wet snow, and wind? You wouldn't believe. I could hardly see the curb-stones on Lexington Avenue."

Laura did as she was told.

"But to the moment at hand. My dear, I have some unsettling news for you."

"Is it about Mama?"

Isabella Bentivengo Ciardi straightened her spine and fixed Laura with a steel pin of an expression. "I've told you if there is ever any news I will not keep it from you. There is no news."

That was all that mattered; nothing else mattered. Then Nonna said, "We have found you a finishing school."

"I don't want to go back to school. I hate school."

"You are too young to make up your own mind about that. In any case, it's against the law for us to keep you home merely because your friends despise you."

"They don't bother to despise me, I'm not worth the effort. And they aren't my friends. They just think I'm an idiot. They laugh at me. I'm not going back there."

"Your grandfather and I are not so blind even if we wear the bifocals. We see. We have been talking to Monsignor and to Mother Saint Boniface. They have found an ideal spot for you. If you finish three semesters there, this school will agree to give you the certificate. Diploma, I think it's called. A small win, Laura, but it is a win."

"Will I have to take the subway? I don't like it downtown."

"It is not within the reach of the subway," said

Nonna, cautiously. In the best of times Laura's grandmother had an uncertain grasp of the subway map. The hesitation, however, didn't sound good. "It's in Montreal," continued Nonna. "We'll go there by train."

Laura knew she was sometimes slow to pick up what was going on. But: "Mon-tre-*al*? Not the one in Canada?"

"That's the only Montreal there is, anyway that I know about."

"You don't mean I have to live there?"

"*Carissima,*" said Nonna. "You can't stay here hiding in your bedroom, worrying your grandfather and me to an early grave."

It's too late for you to enjoy an early grave, you're as old as sin.

"I don't hide," said Laura. "And I'm not going. I can't. I don't know how to speak Canadian."

"They speak French and English in Montreal. Luckily this is an English-speaking school, though the nuns will try to teach to you some French. We'd all rather it be Italian, but the Italians didn't colonize Quebec."

Laura said through her tears, "Nonna, this can't be happening. I've changed my mind. I'll go back to Driscoll. I was out of line but I'm ready now."

"Driscoll won't have you back," said Nonna the know-it-all. Was that a smirk?

"I'll go to public school."

"That would be worse. I've asked around. The Ladies' Auxiliary agrees. A girl with hardly any academic interests, she needs a finishing school." Nonna fished a letter from her pocketbook. "The institution has written me. They can take you after the first of the year. It's called the Academy of—"

"I don't need to know what it's called because I'm not going."

Nonna stood up. "I'm afraid you are, my dear. I can't go into the whys and how-comes now. It's in your best interest. After what happened at Driscoll and your grandfather's worries, not to mention your poor mother—well, I'm not getting any younger, either. On Monday you go tell your first graders that it's your last day."

"I don't know how to do that."

"This is precisely what I mean," said Nonna. "You are sixteen years old. Old enough to take charge of your life. You need finishing, and Nonno and I seem not to be up to the job."

"I'm fifteen. Mary Bernice can teach me at home."

"How to boil potatoes? I don't think that's enough."

"She can teach me how to be nice," said Laura, nearly spitting.

"I am trying to be nice," said Nonna, attempting at a soft expression that succeeded only in making her look like an executioner enjoying a daydream. "If I'm failing, that's more proof that we can't do this any longer. Laura, we want the best for you. We always have done. It's been how many years since your mother—"

Laura wasn't about to let Nonna go into that. If there was no news from her mother, there was no point in flapping about the subject. "May I be excused?" she asked.

"We'll talk about it at dinner. It won't be so bad, you'll see."

"I'm not in for dinner," said Laura.

"What do you mean by that?" Nonna's look of tyranny returned. "I haven't given you any permission—"

"I'm going to church with Mary Bernice."

Nonna pursed her lips. She knew she'd been outmaneuvered. "In this snow?" she began, but gave up. Church trumped everything else. "Well, pray for me, too."

Laura plunged down the back stairs into the kitchen, which was half-sunk in the ground. The high windows above the sink looked out into the bereaved backyard. Snow was frosting the dead leaves clumped outside the windows.

Tomorrow's pot roast sizzled in a pressure cooker.

Its little valve made a lonely jingle against the heavy pot lid. On top of the cookbooks, the cat opened one eye and uttered a monotonic comment. "Shut up, Garibaldi," said Laura. Mary Bernice must be in the bathroom. Or no—now she could hear her—the cook was upstairs in the front hall, talking over life and its limitations with the workers.

Generally Laura wasn't allowed to make conversation with tradespeople, but she turned around and went upstairs. The front door was closing. John Greenglass and Sam, Sam what's-he-called, *Sam-I-am,* were just gone. Mary Bernice was stowing the drop cloths in the hall closet beneath Nonna's dripping boots. In the ceiling, the wet plaster had been torn out; only lathes and strapping showed. "Did they take the owl?" asked Laura. "I wanted to keep it. It belongs here." She ran to the door.

"You'll catch your death," said Mary Bernice, without conviction.

In her stockinged feet Laura descended the steps of the brownstone to the slate paving stones of the sidewalk. Van Pruyn Place was a dead end, and there was only one way John's blue truck could drive out. There it was at the corner, halted at the stop sign, blinker on, ready to turn onto East End Avenue. The rush hour traffic should hold the truck in time for Laura to reach it. And do—what? Say what? "Give me the owl." "Let me in." "Take me away." "Come back."

But before she could get there, John's truck eased out and turned, lost in the stream of taxis and cars and trucks.

Laura stood on the pavement, shivering. The snow circled like carnival ticker tape. All of the great city around her was engaged and alive, and Laura alone stood shoeless in the snow outside the warmly lit brownstones. The loneliness she felt was so keen it was almost elegant. It cut her. Every snowflake on her bare arms had steel blades. There was no future and no past in such immediate pain.

"Are you barmy, get in here before the devil gives you germs," called Mary Bernice from the area near the rubbish bins. "And you wonder why everyone frets about you so."

Laura turned at last. The wind off the East River tore harder against her. A grade-school boy in a jacket three sizes too large for him slipped in the slush as he ran across the street with a fistful of Christmas greens in his palm. He righted himself without falling, though. He must be on his way to a school musicale, for he slid on down to the corner, singing something to himself about the holly and the ivy, and the running of the deer.

3

In the evenings, the kitchen was warmer than the attic. Mary Bernice was half through her own meal. "There's a nice slice of Sunbeam in the bread bin with your name on it, Miss Laura." Laura got the bread. There was no name written on it. She knew there wouldn't be but she turned it over to check the other side. Real butter tonight, not margarine. The hard butter tore the bread into soft white clumps. Laura ate the morsels like hors d'oeuvres.

"Why do they have to send me away?" she asked the cook.

Mary Bernice hadn't heard about this. She put her spoon down. "You've mistook something, I'm thinking. Where on earth do they want to put you?"

"Some prison in Canada."

"I'm sure you've gotten the wrong end of the stick, Laura. Your grandparents have their notions, but I doubt they mean to do anything of the sort. They're just fretting about that hole in the ceiling. Sure, aren't they besides themselves with getting ready, and them relations. Give your elders and betters a little room."

Laura was mopey. She dawdled over the pasta fazool that Mary Bernice had set before her. "I don't know why they are so jittery over a stupid dinner party. It's Nonna's sister coming for a visit, not the Pope."

"Families are mysteries. You of all people should know that," said Mary Bernice, a little belligerently. But Laura didn't want to consider her own family. She turned her shoulder away from Mary Bernice to indicate indifference. Facing the little room off the kitchen, where Mary Bernice sometimes slept instead of returning to her husband in Stuyvesant Heights, Laura saw Mary Bernice's coat and hat folded neatly on the bed. "Are you going home tonight after church?" she asked the cook.

"It's Ted's bingo night, so no. But I'm still hoping to take in the evening Mass. I prefer Guardian Angel in Chelsea, as I have a devotion to my own dear guardian, but not in weather like this. Queen of Angels will do in a pinch. I'll hop the bus."

Laura said, "I've changed my mind. I'll come with

you. I need to get out of the house. I'm through talking to them for good. They don't listen anyway."

Mary Bernice winked at Laura. "I'll sort it out for you with mister and missus, shall I? We won't be able to take Holy Communion, having eaten so recently, but tomorrow's weather may be worse, and the Lord will understand." She stomped upstairs to make the arrangements. Laura waited for her, huddling inside the basement door that let out under the front stoop. The cat wreathed itself about Laura's boots like a sooty spirit of chimneys past, yellowish eyes narrowing in its grey face.

"Saints and celebrities, but you must have really given them a go," said Mary Bernice. "If you've nothing else to pray for tonight, you can ask forgiveness for rudeness, I'm guessing. The missus was crying a little and old Ovid had set a copy of *Life* magazine on top of his bowl to keep the soup warm, he said, while he was looking through his hi-fi record albums. I think they weren't talking to each other. Marriage is like that, more often than not. Now you stay put, kitty, or you'll be sorry."

Though they could still hear the moist industrial hum of traffic on FDR Drive, the snowy world was more hush than rush. On the crosstown streets the traffic had already thinned. Perhaps everyone but Laura had known a storm was coming, and had gotten home early. "You're smart to stay over tonight," she said.

"Himself will be glad to have a quiet night at home without my complaining, sure enough. I'd take a vacation from meself, too, if I knew how to book it."

They crossed several blocks and ran toward the next bus as it pulled to the stop. It was like a lighted tank of seawater rolling through the snowy gloaming. From outside, the riders were glazed with wet halos, but inside they all seemed to be on morphine, as if they expected never to get home again. Laura snagged a window seat and Mary Bernice settled in next to her and found her rosary. She didn't care for public transport; she used the rosary as a distraction and as a defense against uninvited conversation.

Laura watched the storefronts pass. The Rexall windows were particularly colorful, with their stacked displays of Lavoris, Old Spice, and whatnot. Most of the stores had their iron grates pulled already.

Mary Bernice said that Our Lady Queen of Angels was in the East 110s. Laura knew how the streets worked but rarely bothered to count them, as they counted themselves so correctly. At 91st Laura watched a lady's umbrella blow inside out; the pedestrian pitched the thing in the gutter and sloshed on. The night seemed bedeviled with potential catastrophe, but here they were at church at last, so trouble would have to wait outside in the cold.

Laura didn't have much feeling for Mass itself. Who could? She wasn't expected to understand the Latin. It was a secret language, holiness in code. She read the prayers off the laminated cards in the pews—"*Confiteor Dei omnipotenti*"—(Confess your sins, murmured Mary Bernice helpfully). The congregation droned like zombies. The oddly clinical scent of beeswax candles laced itself into a mothbally fug of stone-pressed cold air.

In stained glass high above the altar, the Archangel Gabriel slid into the world. He held a lily in his hand, as if to offer it to the Virgin. She was examining her nails and paying him no attention. Perhaps she was shy. Perhaps the angel was speaking in Latin and the Virgin knew only English.

Finally the priest ascended to the pulpit and began to address the congregation in English. "Pay attention now, I'm going to grill you about it on the bus home," growled Mary Bernice. So Laura tried to concentrate. She went back and forth between the words and the angel in the window, stitching everything together, like pictures and words in a storybook she read to the first graders at the after-school program at Driscoll.

"Well," said Mary Bernice on the way home, "did

you spend the entirety of Holy Mass thinking about yourself, yourself, yourself?"

"I did not," said Laura, wondering what made Mary Bernice so crusty sometimes. Faith could be an angry urge in the cook. "Well, not the whole time."

"Miss Laura Ciardi. We go to Mass for courage in our trials. I know you've had a bad afternoon and you're feeling punky. Your faith can inoculate you against despair. Come along now, what did you take in?"

This was almost like being asked to cough up the natural resources of Brazil or the significant rivers of the African continent. Answers in words came so slowly. "He said angels were messengers. That the word *angel* means messenger in some rusty old language. That angels were a sign of, um, grace, and that Mary was one very lucky young virgin to win the big prize. Zip-a-dee-doo-dah. Also our guardian angels are invisible but this guy—Gabriel—came down from heaven and delivered a message, like someone from the telephone and telegraph company."

Mary Bernice started to laugh a little despite herself. "I'm sorry I asked. The lesson of the sermon, listen to me, Laura, was simply that Advent is a time of holding your breath. He is coming, said the angel. The salvation of the world is coming. Hold on, everybody, and expect the unexpected. At least," she said with a roll of her shoulders, "that's what I got out of it. Father isn't always easy to follow, with that accent. I think he's from West Africa. But he says a nice Mass, for my money."

"Is the owl from our ceiling like some angel sliding down on a slat of light?"

"Beware your imagination, Laura. Occasion of sin if you don't look out. An owl is not an angel. A bird in the house is a sign that someone will die soon. Nothing more than that."

They sat in silence the rest of the ride. The bus was emptier, sleepier. No other vehicles on the streets now but taxis.

"I wouldn't mind an angel," said Laura, almost to herself.

"Everyone wants to get something, everyone has something to give," replied Mary Bernice. "Even the rich want their Christmas presents, even the poor want to give their mite. Aren't I just after saying to our cousin Sheila in the Bronx that I wanted to give a nice coat to the clothing drive for the poor. 'Ooh,' says our Sheila, 'I'll take that coat off your hands, I like it.' I said, 'It's bloody Christmas, Sheila. I want to give this to the poor, not to the cheap and miserly. Buy your own damn coat.'"

In the most basic of terms, Laura knew that she herself was not actually poor. She had a coat from Macy's in Herald Square, full price, not picked up at a sale. It was pearl blue edged with a rolled white cord that finished in braidwork around the buttonholes. She had seen in the pews three or four people who wore the plastic sleeves from dry cleaning around their shoulders to keep the snow off their threadbare jackets. Poor was poor and rich was something else. But she slept in a cold attic room and had no parents to speak of, and virtually no friends. Mary Bernice didn't count. So while this wasn't poverty, it was some cousin to poverty.

4

When she went upstairs, she saw the light was still on in the parlor and the door was open a crack. “Is that you, Laurita?” called her grandfather. “Come down and see us before you go to bed.” He used his sweet-touch voice. Somehow she resented him most when he was trying to be thoughtful.

“I have a headache, I’ll see you tomorrow.” She was up on her own floor now, and closed the bathroom door to avoid hearing any argument.

She was still thinking about ways of being rich and poor, and how she had eaten a bowl of pasta fazool for supper and had clean blankets and her own bathroom, even if the sink sported a big crack in it. On the windowsill she had two kinds of shampoo and a bottle of spray to hold her do in place. But here she was lying in the dark again. She whisked her forefingers along her closed eyelashes, removing damp. She heard the sound of footsteps in the hall below.

"Laura?" It was her grandmother, wheezing from the effort of stairs. "You can't be asleep, I just heard the toilet flush. This last flight is too steep for me so come where I can see you. I want to talk to you."

The struggle over being obedient or being willful. Laura got up and walked in her slip to the top of the stairs and stood there sullenly with her arms folded over her.

"I know you need some time to get used to everything new," said Nonna. She had made it up the first two steps. A world record. "It's normal. I want to talk to you some more about this tomorrow. We're all going to ten o'clock Mass and I have Sodality afterward. Nonno has to count the collections as usual, so we'll go over all this Montreal business at lunchtime when we get back. *Capisci?*"

"Mary Bernice thinks I caught a cold being out tonight. At *church*."

Nonna grunted like a cavewoman. "Terrific. Well, get some rest and we'll see how you feel in the morning."

Laura coughed stagily and tried to change the subject. "I'm going to stay home tomorrow and have Mary Bernice teach me how to smoke a cigarette."

But Nonna just laughed at that. "I think she's leaving after she makes the morning coffee. But if she stays, have her give you a glass or two of beer while you're at it. If you're going to go to hell, take the express train. Now, seriously, if you're sick, I'll see you tomorrow at lunch. It's the pot roast. Don't forget to say your prayers."

"I said them at church."

"Say them again. Insurance."

Laura's silence was, in her opinion anyway, both belligerent and magnificent.

Nonna continued cagily. "You could always join us at church after Mass and do Sodality with me. If you feel better by then."

Sodality of the Virgin Mary was extra-credit rosaries chanted by a phalanx of old women wearing black lace veils. "No thank you. Good night."

"Yes," said Nonna, turning around and fastening her hand upon the rail. She never said *good night* back; one remark seemed to serve for the whole household.

Nonna huffed away, landing both feet on each step for security before proceeding to the next. Her broad back made a perfect target. But all Laura could put her hands on quickly was a can of Elegance hairspray, and probably it would just bounce off Nonna without her noticing. It wasn't worth it.

Laura returned to her room and lay down so she could be poor and cold on the Upper East Side. But then she got up. She was remembering something the priest had said about *Veni, Veni, Emmanuel.* O come, o come, Emmanuel. She went to her window. The cord in the sash was broken but there was a piece of wood on the sill that she used to prop the window up on hot summer nights. She used it now. Never mind the cold air.

The wrought iron railings that had kept small children safe, back when Laura's room was a nursery for some long-gone New York family, were leaning up like iron fencing in the box room next door. John Greenglass and Sam-Whoever-He-Is had taken them down that morning so they could climb out to repair the stonework and fix the leak.

The sky was flat with snowlight. She could smell balsam, and a hint of the sea on the rising wind, and something like sauerkraut. She stayed there for quite a few minutes, her chin propped in her hands.

O come, o come, Emmanuel, sang the girl.

5

The next morning set in, bleak as a diagnosis. The snow had stopped falling but the wind kept it unsettled, rushing it against the windows as Laura rambled about the empty house. It was well past ten before she accepted that Sam and John weren't going to show up today. Of course: Sunday. Without realizing it, she had hoped that she would be home with them, and nobody else fussing about. She couldn't name for herself what she wanted, so she tried to tell it as if she were a character in some story of her own life.

The girl had wanted—well, company?

At last she put on her everyday coat and let herself out the utility entrance. She headed west, which was the only way to go unless you wanted to throw yourself in the East River. She crossed East End Avenue and continued on toward the park, but at Fifth Avenue she decided to head downtown to look at the decorated store windows. She walked to keep warm underneath the low clouds, now a gritty caramel color. Foot traffic was steady. Nothing stopped New Yorkers from getting their Sunday papers and coffees, and their bagels in white wax bags.

Once in a while she thought about Montreal, but there wasn't much to think about it. It was up in the Arctic somewhere, up past Albany and Troy. She would be stationed there like a soldier at a hardship post. At least here she felt like a player with a walk-on part in her own life and times. In Montreal she would only be one of the stage mob saying "rhubarb rhubarb."

The ordinary world asserted itself through a smorgasbord of aromas. Hot air from a dryer vent. A sizzle of onions. A reek of roasting chestnuts and nearly scorched salt pretzels from a pushcart tended by an old woman in a babushka.

Things got more evened out, even a little perfumed, on Fifth Avenue. She kept walking, lost in her thoughts or what passed for thoughts, until she caught sight of herself in the windows of Scribner's. A cellophane cutout of a girl. Polar gusts flickered snow-dust around her. The wind tore her long, irresolutely colored hair out from her head scarf, an insult of apparel Laura was obliged to wear on Sundays whether in church or not. She tried to catch her eyes glancingly in the window to see if she looked as stupid as she felt. Coal-dark and judgmental, her eyes were forming some opinion about her that she couldn't decipher.

"Someone happy about herself," said a big black lady in a striped yellow coat large enough to button around an ambulance. She was dragging a shopping bag bristling with about a dozen frothy heads of celery.

"Sorry," said Laura. She was in the way and inched over.

"Celery soup for lunch at the Rescue Mission, and I'm late. My bus don't show. Take some celery and lighten my load, or get out of my way, I got a stove to park myself in front of."

Laura ducked back and Celery Lady trudged on. The celery was getting frozen, but maybe soup didn't care about that.

Crossing Fifth Avenue, Laura headed back uptown so the wind would be at her back. Then she walked around Rockefeller Center. On Sixth Avenue near Radio City Music Hall she visited her favorite decorations, bas-reliefs carved in sand-toned stone above the doors at street level. A naked woman on the back of a swan. A Pegasus. A one-armed man hoisted aloft by an eagle. Well, he had a second arm but it was mostly hidden behind the outstretched wing. The ornamentations of the heavy limestone buildings were all about flying. She ignored the great ridiculous Christmas tree, too large to love, really sort of monstrous. She preferred the loose-limbed, gold-plated young god below it, nearly naked even in this weather, sprawled upon his ring of golden orbit.

The ice-skating rink opened up beneath him. Laura sidled along the railing, gliding on her elbows. From above, she watched couples and singles on the ice. Beside her, a man in a stiff black hat with a feather in it was complaining about the waltzy music to a younger woman who might have been his daughter or his secretary or maybe a baby sister.

"Shut up and let me listen to the music," replied his companion. "It's pretty. It's all fairy-tale and princesses."

"You're the princess, you know that? But you should get yourself some better taste in tunes. This stuff gives me a pain in my wiener schnitzel. Gimme a bit of Dean Martin and a Scotch on the rocks any day. 'Fly Me to the Moon,' why doncha."

"At this hour? Herbie, you're the rat's ass, hands off me, we're supposed to be at church, I told my ma. Someone could see us."

Laura made sure her eyes were facing away but she kept listening. The music surged in tempered waves. "Herbie, get your hand outa my pocket, I might have an open mousetrap in there."

Probably not father and daughter, Laura thought, but then, how would she know?

She was reluctant to leave the music but the self-approval of people braving the winds before Christmas was getting on her nerves. She scurried uptown, crossing just at 58th to glance in the windows of F. A. O. Schwarz. Stuffed animals drowning in tinsel. Then she veered back across Fifth Avenue and into Central Park, with its glistening, wet-sugar paths and its happy goofy dogs and their hungover owners. The outcroppings of schist—thank you Mrs. Mulvaney in fourth grade, for schist, and gneiss, and limestone—were sprayed with diamond gleam. Two young men walked by holding hands until they saw Laura looking. Don't mind me, what's wrong with brotherly affection, she thought. But she wouldn't really know about that either.

This was the great mystery of the city in which she lived. It was so filled with variety that she had always trusted, somehow, that she would find her own available place in it. A perch, like that of any bird. A hidey-hole like the one that little white owl had found. There was enough otherliness here to have room for Laura. Surely?

But being moved to the care of nuns in Montreal—that couldn't be good. That didn't sound like roosting, but like migration. Or banishment. Or jail.

She passed pigeons scavenging for grain spilled from the feed buckets of the carriage horses. Crossed some widths where the wind growled with turbid force. Paced the stately alley of leafless elms, ended up at the snowy steps descending to the drained water basin of Bethesda Fountain. She approached the angel statue with its flared wings and its loving but blank expression. She tried to find the exact place to stand in which she could meet the angel's eyes and be recognized. But either the angel was blind, like justice, or Laura was just not worth noticing. Into the corridors of wind and time the angel looked, seeing what Laura could not see, seeing anything and maybe everything but Laura herself. Seeing the blank space that made up Laura.

Someone was urging his kids to climb over the basin's stone edge and stand and face his big box camera. "The Cohn family," said the dad. "Three Cohns in the fountain! Smile, kids." The kids, dad-rich, smiled at him.

6

Waiting at the light at 63rd and Madison, Laura turned her head to keep from being splashed by a taxi grinding to a halt. Grey water dashed upon her coat. Looking up at the sound of someone snickering, she saw Donna Flotarde a few steps away. Donna's parents were behind her a step or two, arm in arm like real people, smiling. Donna was hissing, "She's the one—Ciardi's Fine Foods, remember I told you?" When Donna realized she'd been overheard, she winced out a fake smile. "Oh, *hi,* Laura," said Donna Flotarde. Laura had no words with which to reply, but Mr. and Mrs. Flotarde said, "Merry Christmas, honey," as if they were all cousins or something, and the Flotardes picked their way past in single file.

Two storefronts on this side of Madison were packed

from doorway to curb with Christmas trees for sale, leaving only a narrow path through the green woods. The Flotardes disappeared in the temporary forest.

"Hi, Donna," said Laura finally, after they were too distant to hear her. Laura wondered how far along the next block they would get before Donna Flotarde would fill her parents in on the story of why Laura had been expelled from Driscoll. It was so stupid, still; Laura could hardly bear to think about it. Instead, she looked at the taxi, which had dumped onto the pavement four irate ladies in Sunday church clothes.

"We going to heaven, but not in your taxi, you want to kill us all before we get to Salvation Chapel? No, I don't think *so,* Mister Manny." The chief church lady threw a few bills in the taxi window. "More than one cab working this avenue, and anyways we can walk and hallelujah at the same time if we got to." The women stepped out into Madison with four gloved hands lifted in formation, alerting the next taxi driver to their immediate need.

Back to the dead-end lane of Van Pruyn Place at last. Nonno and Nonna weren't home from church yet. In the warm light of the kitchen with its contact paper wallpaper and the lampshade featuring a parade of jolly fat cooks, Laura was, if not happy, at least alone and safe. Mary Bernice was a mere ghost of Jean Naté in the pantry, a trace of personality among the Christmas cloves and cinnamon. The cook had probably taken some gingerbread to give to her husband, Ted, who worked Sunday mornings in a Thruway tollbooth too far away, Nyack or somewhere.

Laura filled the kettle and pulled some loose mint tea from the canister and milk from the Frigidaire. After checking to make sure there were no peeping Toms in the back alley, she rolled off her tights and hung them over the radiator, which was hissing in a jazzy way. Garibaldi sidled over to sniff the fabric and to claw at it, but Laura made the *pssst* sound, and the cat ran off.

She turned on the radio, a red plastic dome-top device seething with emphysema. She'd get in trouble if she fiddled with the dial, so she tolerated what came on. The program was running seasonal. A dulcet voice introduced a carol Laura remembered having sung in the school Christmas pageant a few years ago.

In the bleak midwinter
Frosty winds made moan
Earth stood hard as iron
Water like a stone.
Snow had fallen, snow on snow,
Snow on snow,

In the bleak midwinter
Long time ago.

Laura settled into Mary Bernice's chair. She sniffed at the tea and let the aroma become both warmth and wetness upon her cheeks. It felt like tears, though generally tears didn't taste of peppermint.

A rare moment of—something—continued to fall over her. Outside, frosty winds were making moan again. A branch dropped on the metal palings that divided the Ciardi yard from that of old Mrs. Steenhauser the next street over.

The world wanted so hard to be poetic, and really it was only stupid.

Everything falling through the air. Baby owls, branches, snow on snow on snow. Airplanes. A Bobby Vee record hurtling down Stairwell B at Driscoll School.

Where would she fall from in the end, she wondered—how high need she climb to find out how steep is the fatal fall?

She'd been here about five years now, more or less. Ovid and Isabella Ciardi were growing old as she was growing up. Laura could do the counting backward and figure it out perfectly if she wanted, but she was ashamed still to be using her fingers to count on.

This house on Van Pruyn Place. Home and yet not home; more a *here* than a home. Even with her own room upstairs, and a blue chenille bedspread, and a nightstand with a picture of her brother Marco on it. Her own bathroom with its pink tiles and black trim. She didn't even have to close the door to her bathroom if she didn't want, not since the governess left a few years ago. Nobody came upstairs anymore.

Not very like home, but the most home she had had for the past years, ever since her mother. Since her mother.

But she wouldn't allow that thought to fall upon her. She twitched her head and, Sunday or not, said, "Damnation."

If she could tell what she had done, maybe she could think of a way to undo it. If she could write it out? But probably not—she hadn't been able to produce a paragraph about herself and how she had spent her summer, not once in five years. Something blocked her words from escaping through the pen.

Still, she *could* see Maxine Sugargarten. Weird stuck-up alluring Maxine. Laura could see herself at the top of the flight of steps, holding Maxine's record album in its sleeve. Maxine had been going on for ten days about how her brother was coming home for Christmas. She had gotten him Bobby Vee's record album called *Take Good Care of My Baby.* It wasn't such a terrific album, and wasn't even new anymore, but Maxine had been carting it around the halls and showing it off and talking about her big brother coming home until Laura could stand it no longer.

Put the disaster in order, she announced to herself. If you can arrange it in your mind as it happened, maybe you can predict the next step forward. Maybe even manage to take that step. If there is one.

There was always a before to every story. "What is past is prologue," fluted Miss Parsley in Composition, period three every Monday morning. "Who have you become over the weekend? Who are you *now*? Tell me something that happened to you since seventh period Friday. What happened. Make me see it! Let me be able to hand your paragraph straight to a certain Mr. Alfred Hitchcock. Supply so many visual details and human gestures that he can set up a camera and record your incident without delay. Short is good! But do it right away! Be readable now. And remember your ending: it's *most* important. What does your experience *mean*? What does it signify? Change, growth, understanding, realization?"

Laura could tell her first paragraph to herself any

time of the day or night. She was good at looking and seeing. She just couldn't write it down. As for the conclusions, forget it. What things meant was impossible to guess or say, even in her secret soliloquies.

Garibaldi kneaded his way into Laura's lap. She began to tell it as if she were the point of the story, but even Garibaldi yawned, as if it would be a stretch to expect him to care much about her travails.

Gym. Second period, Monday morning. At the end of the volleyball game, the girl had plunged into the locker room with the rest of the team. They had twelve minutes to shower, change, and be in English two flights up. The last one in the door of the English room at the start of third period on Mondays had to read aloud her "Past Is Prologue" paragraph. So the girl made sure she was never last. Ever.

Maxine Sugargarten blasting reports about her big brother returning from basic training for Christmas. Donna Flotarde as some sort of cheer squad behind her most of the time, and then Aarathi and Cindy and Mary Colleen O'Cassidy snaking around on the sidelines, too. They'd taken against Laura, to be sure. Oh, yes, long before the locker room, and the stolen record album. In the gym, in the halls, in assembly, everywhere.

Back when there were boys in class it hadn't been so bad. Laura had been too quiet to pester. Boys equal noise. But after promotion from sixth grade at Driscoll, the boys had to go to Prentiss-Drake. In seventh grade, Driscoll became all girls. And once the camouflage of boys was cleared away, Laura's status among her classmates devolved into being a sort of *cafona* from the back of beyond. Brought to light in order to make the other girls feel good about themselves. Laura, a half-orphan, stuck in a house with those ridiculous ancient Italian people.

Garibaldi looked up at her accusatorily. *You had friends,* said the cat. *Don't say you didn't.*

But she didn't. The cat was wrong. Sure, two fourth-grade girls had looked up to Laura when she'd helped out in the art room that one time. They'd followed her around in the cafeteria for a while.

"On Saturday afternoon I went on a date with my boyfriend to see *Birdman of Alcatraz* at the rep," said one of her volleyball teammates as they rushed into the shower last Monday morning. "We wanted to see *To Kill a Mockingbird* but it isn't out till next week. What did you do over the weekend, Laura? Did you hang out with your fourth-grade fan club at the soda fountain? What fun!"

"Shut up," said Laura, quietly; she could hardly even hear herself.

Usually she was so eager to be the first one to English that she skipped the showers, barely swabbing under her arms with a damp paper towel before getting dressed. But the girls in the locker room were feeling gangstery, maybe from holiday high spirits. As Laura turned to reach for her camisole, Aarathi opened the top of her liquid Prell and gave it a squeeze. Green globs jumped on Laura's hair and shoulder blades. "Oh," said Aarathi, nearly sneezing with joy. "What a disaster! So *sorry*, Laura. Quick, you have time to shower."

She had no choice, and the other girls were half-dressed already. If she didn't hurry, she'd be last. Then she'd have to admit out loud in Parsley's class that she did nothing on the weekend but go to church, and with her elderly grandparents. Her imagination was rich, but her life straitjacketed, and panic seized up her mind in the best of times.

She had careered into the shower stall and turned on the hot water. Her hair was goopy. She snapped the curtain shut and powered up the hot. She could still make it; she was faster than everyone. Not until later did she remember the sound of a plastic-seated bench dragging across the floor tiles of the next stall. After her ski accident at Killington, Doll Pettigrew had been using the bench to balance herself in the shower. Laura should have noticed the scrape.

This was the part she couldn't bear to picture. Someone—was it Maxine, was it Aarathi, Donna, Cindy?—someone had climbed on the bench in the next shower stall and peered over the wall at naked Laura Ciardi in the shower. Laura's eyes were closed because the shampoo was in her hair. She kept trying to rinse it out but the suds wouldn't go; they were the Sorcerer's Apprentice of liquid Prell soapsuds. They kept coming and coming. She would be late. There was giggling. Finally she tore the curtain open. The other girls were all dressed and dashing for the locker room door.

She was alone, dripping. Her clothes were where she had left them except her training bra and her underpants, nowhere. Her hair was more rubber than human.

The bell rang as she skidded into the doorway. "Oh, something *new,*" said Miss Parsley. "Last in, first up, Laura! We haven't heard from you all year. Slap right to work, girls! Deliver your weekend, tell me what happened and what it signified, and that means we are new people, we are ready, girls, to be ourselves in a new way for this whole new week, girls! You have ten minutes."

Her classmates had set her up, out of no other impulse than meanness and boredom. They wanted to see her suffer.

The girl turned and looked around at the class as Joan of Arc might have done, inspecting the arrangement of kindling at her feet. It was braided like a wreath, and she was the upright pillar of wax in the middle, ready for the match.

(Oh, that was good. Laura sat up in Mary Bernice's chair and said it again to herself.)

She was the upright pillar of wax in the middle of the wreath of kindling, turning like Joan of Arc might have done, to inspect her murderers. "Better get your pen out, we can't wait to hear about your weekend," sniggered one of the girls. Miss Parsley didn't catch the sarcasm. The girl asked to go to the bathroom. "You've just come from the gym," said Miss P. "My hair is still sticky, it wouldn't wash out," said the girl, raising a hank as an exhibit, dropping it with disgust. "That's Italiano for you: greasy," murmured a back-seater. "Back in four minutes, and you're still on deck for this assignment," said Miss P.

"We all want to hear what you've been up to."
"Hear it and see it," someone snorted. "Show us everything. Why not bare your soul, since you've already bared your behind?"

The girls didn't take against Laura Ciardi in the locker room because she had done anything to them. Except ignore them, perhaps. They took against her because they could. Because Laura stood out the most, which conferred a practical normality to all the others. Laura with no parents. Laura with no brother to come home at Christmas. No boyfriend. And a history of belligerence if pushed.

Last Monday, during third period, Laura had lingered in the girls' room as long as she dared, hoping Parsley would give up waiting and ask someone else to read her paragraph. As Laura finally was going back to English, she found herself passing Maxine's locker door. Laura checked out the corridors in both directions, peeked in the locker, and found the treasured Bobby Vee album wedged in at an angle—slanting above Maxine's stash of illegal makeup. Laura had lifted the album out and closed the metal locker door without making any noise.

But what to do with it? It was too wide to carry around with her schoolbooks and notebooks. Luckily she had worn a big old cardigan of Nonno's to school that day because the heat in the library was on the fritz. Into the wooly brown sweater she wrapped Maxine's present for her Big Brother Sugargarten—his name was Spike or something—and tucked it under her arm with her other books. More sloppy than usual, but who looked at Laura Ciardi enough to notice?

Her campaign to avoid having to write something and read it aloud had worked, but the impromptu theft had come to light by lunchtime. Maxine Sugargarten was sobbing in the school cafeteria so dramatically that Miss Adenoid, or whatever her name was, the school nurse, had to be summoned. "He's my *brother*," gasped Maxine Sugargarten, as if she were talking about Bobby Vee and not Spike Sugargarten. "And he's been off at basic training for months! And we've been writing letters about this stupid Bobby Vee album, and it is a personal *tribute* to my loving friendship with my *brother*!"

"If anyone knows anything about this missing LP," said Mr. Grackowicz over the public address system, "please bring such information to the attention of the front office. And I might add that for someone to snitch someone else's Christmas present is not a very nice thing to do in this season of peace on earth, goodwill to men. End of transmission." Mr. G. had been in the navy.

After lunch, Laura hunched in the cold library with her grandfather's sweater folded under her chair. She was supposed to be doing a biology project on anatomy. The subject was bones, which was mostly copying drawings from the acetate overlays in the *World Book Encyclopedia*. Laura had asked if she could do a drawing of a bird wing rather than a human arm, and label all the parts. It would still be a reticulated diagram. Miss Frobisher had held out for the human arm as being more pertinent to the subject of Human Anatomy, Fall Semester. Laura had thought that was small-minded of her because we all came from birds way back. Back when we could fly.

The human arm was repulsive, really, when you thought about it. That coronoid process, and the shading where the ulna turned. How slender, how easily broken. The very airiness of a wing so much more useful—more flexible, more giving.

When the bell rang she saw she had only doodled seagulls flapping above a single-line horizon. The Human Bone had failed to emerge any further than an outline. Laura had slapped her stuff together and headed up toward Remedial Reading.

The luck of high school traffic patterns brought Maxine Sugargarten and Donna Flotarde heading down the steps of Staircase B just as Laura was starting up. Maxine's face looked like a Halloween fright mask, tracks of tears betraying her illicit eyeliner. Maxine was dragging her heels. By now everyone in the school knew Maxine was Trauma Case Number One for the day, and she'd be given some leeway. But Donna Flotarde had too many demerits to be late again, so she was leaping ahead. Finding herself alone with Maxine, Laura made her big mistake. "I am *so sorry* about your lost record, Maxine."

Maxine halted at the landing. She was just one of the pretty thugs who plagued Laura, she wasn't any kind of friend. Laura hurried a little to pass her. "I just mean, you have a brother, that's the good part, I guess," Laura said, pausing at the top.

"Of course it's the good part, but my surprise is ruined," snapped Maxine.

"I mean at least he's coming home."

"What is that supposed to mean?"

Oh, she'd gone too far. "Nothing. Wow for your brother, wow. Great. See ya. I'm going to be late for Pretzel." (Miss Prelutsky.)

Maxine's snake-eyes had narrowed. "You're awfully interested in my brother."

"I'm not at all interested in any brothers of yours."

"You never even met him."

"How could I meet him, he's at basic training you said. I don't care about him."

"What do you have under your sweater? Laura? Did you take my Bobby Vee?"

"You're medically off your rocker, Maxine." Laura hugged the sweater to her bosom. The second bell had rung and they were alone in the stairwell, Maxine still paused at the halfway point, and Laura frozen on high alert at the top landing.

"Wave out your sweater, Laura Ciardi, or I'll tell Mr. G. It's just the kind of stupid thing you'd do. Prove you don't have my brother's record album. Show me."

What could she do but live and suffer. Laura clopped her science book and her other books and binder on the floor. Opposite her, across the stairwell, the tall double-sashed window was partly open. It had been stuck that way since the summer. The gap up top was about a foot or so. Laura said, "Take good care of my baby," and then, "I don't have your stupid LP, see?" and with a flick of her wrist she sent the square record sleeve skirling toward the open part of the window. Maxine could find it in the alley with the cigarette butts and greasy pizza-slice papers. But a downdraft or some other perversity interfered, and the LP became a guided missile. Its thin edge smashed hard against the bridge of Maxine Sugargarten's nose. It took good care of her baby squirmy face. There was a trip to Miss Adenoid's office, and the emergency room, and Maxine's precious nose had had to be cauterized. And on Tuesday morning Laura came back to school in her Sunday coat from Macy's and she sat outside Mr. Grackowicz's office while Nonna and Nonno went inside to bargain for her.

The slatted bench was hard. The school secretary was adding up packets of lunch money and coming to different sums each time, and swearing softly under her minted breath. Laura tried to eavesdrop between the counting and the swearing.

"She not a girl, she nearly addled," Nonno was saying. His accent betrayed his anxiety; Laura knew he was trying to call her *adult,* not *addled.* "This only play, only fun time, this no assault. We send Sugargartens fat brick Parmigiano and small smoked ham and nice bottle best imported Barolo."

"Also some crystal ginger slices, Mr. Headmaster," added Nonna. "Mountains and molehills, do not mistake them, Mr. Headmaster. Everything is not the Alps. Some things are pimples, not Alps." She was trotting out her Ladies' Auxiliary elocution voice big-time.

Mr. G. had replied in a low tone. Laura couldn't pick out a word.

"She sorry, she write sorry letter, that she can do," said Nonno. "We make her. We help her. She no write but she think sorry. We write, she sign, love, love."

"If they only charged the same for chocolate milk as for white," said the secretary to Laura, "this wouldn't be my weekly migraine."

"I'm not so good at counting, can't help," replied Laura in a whisper, wanting the woman to shut up.

"Of course who forget childhood, it shake everyone, childhood, Mr. Headmaster. *Your* childhood shake you up, you turn into Mr. Headmaster. All good." But the accent was getting stronger. Nonno was losing confidence in his argument. "But she no child no more, she addled. Her father—"

Mr. Grackowicz cleared his throat; he didn't want to hear the family history.

Nonno wouldn't be deterred. "Our only child, Mr. G. In World War Number Two, he fight on our side, Mr. G., on our American side. We already here, we Ciardis, we no Fascist. We come here 1929, just in time for Great Depression, we in line at soup table. First we eat, and when we can, we cook and we serve. We make our way. We Yankee doodles. We fight for American freedom. Laura's papa, he our son. Our son Giuseppe, he fight for freedom in South Pacific Ocean. After war, when he get demobbed, he go join U.S. occupation in Austria. He *die* there, service to his country. Giuseppe Ciardi, buried in American military grave. You can't throw Giuseppe daughter out of your brave free U.S.A. school, not when our Giuseppe he sacrifice his life. Honor our son, Mr. G. *Honor.* His soldier friends they call him Joe. American hero Joe Ciardi, *riposa in pace.*"

Mr. Grackowicz *really* didn't want to hear the full history of the Ciardi family, but once Nonno got started, look out.

"And the mother, Laura's mama, her with only one boy, then *he* go down in crash, Mr. G.! This Marco, this Laura only brother! Laura only one left! Who can blame Laura mama for sickness in head, in heart? I ask you. We know what mama feel, we feel same. Two deaths in ten years, what family is to bear? I ask you! We do what we can to make Laura her leftover child addled. We take her in, we love her Laura, we raise her. We need Laura here. She big, big help in store. I send you box of best Campania blood oranges by special bicycle delivery boy before you leave school today, Mr. G."

Then Mr. G. talked for a long, long time. He was probably reading from reports by other teachers, who had "concerns" about "fitness" and "deportment."

Maybe "fistfights." When the door finally opened and Mr. G. said, "Miss Ciardi, come in here please," Laura could hardly move.

She came to the doorway and wouldn't sit down. "I'm sorry, I said I was sorry," said Laura. "I didn't mean to hit Maxine Sugargarten in the schnozzle."

"That was only the tip of the iceberg, Laura," said Mr. G., shaking his head.

"That's some iceberg," replied Laura, which no one thought was funny. She didn't tell about the locker room ambush earlier that day. It was too awful to say aloud.

"I'll put everything in writing," said Mr. G. "That is how we do it."

"Giuseppe Ciardi, only son, sacrifice for our chosen nation," said Signore Ovid Ciardi, but with failing conviction. "And it come to this."

So it came to this, with Laura sitting in Mary Bernice's chair of a Sunday morning, teetering between a wreck of a high school career and becoming an exile to someplace so far away it might as well be another country. Well, it was, wasn't it? Canada wasn't in New York. The air would be clean and clear and she might die of oxygen poisoning without the rich diesel winds of Manhattan.

She pressed against her sides as if she were showing a doctor where it hurt. But nothing hurt. It just—it just felt.

Everything hurt, actually, except her skin and her bones and muscles. Everything inside her was dry as old spiderweb. She was too young to feel old.

So she was almost relieved now to hear Nonna home from her devotions. The key in the lock, the creak of the old door. "*Madre di Dio,* what are we going to do?" called Nonna. Perhaps she forgot that Mary Bernice was off for the day.

"I'm coming, Nonna," called Laura, dumping the cat on the braided rug laid on top of the linoleum floor. "Mary Bernice is out today."

"The whole house is collapsing," said Nonna. "Everything is collapsing." It did look a wreck. More of the hall ceiling had fallen down while Laura had been stalking the snowy streets. "Mop this up, would you, Laura, you'll find a bucket in Rosa Mendoza's cupboard. If I didn't believe the Christ Child had come to bring us peace and joy, I'd say there was a Christmas plague upon this house."

When Nonno got home, he picked up the phone. "They come back at seven A.M. *domani,*" he then reported. "They find leak, they fix. Tomorrow only wind, no snow. They start on ceiling repair. They say not worry, Bella. They have time and they have smart hands. They good boys. Mrs. Steenhauser give them good notices. They do her back porch steps last summer, spic and span. They finish us up here tomorrow."

"I want a small Negroni before Laura brings out the antipasti and the rice salad," replied Bella Ciardi. "What is the thing the American ladies tell me say? Yes, I remember. 'I can't cope.' How that, Nonno? 'I can't *cope*, get me my Negroni.' I am so up-to-the-minute, no, *caro*?"

7

Laura curled the edge of her blanket in her clenched fingers. Who ever said that the wind howls? That's no howl, thought Laura.

It wasn't a cheery sound, and she tried to tell herself braver than she was.

The dark was full of movement. Tides of night sweeping. The wind howled—

No, not howled.

The wind made a pitchy shriek like a teakettle still a few moments from the boil.

That wasn't bad, that was accurate, that was what it sounded like. Still, the trick of putting herself in the middle of a told tale didn't make her feel any better, for once.

The snow had stopped, though Nonno had said it was expected again by the following evening. Perhaps a heavier fall next time. Laura looked up at the yellow undersides of the clouds. Beveled smudges, vaguely purgatorial.

The girl felt the buzz of inactivity in her breast.

But what did that mean? A buzz of *inactivity*? That was a figure-of-speech thing, she couldn't remember what it was called. Contradiction. A buzz of inactivity. That must be what the primordial ooze felt before the first single-celled animal pulled itself together and decided to crawl toward the seashore for a little sunbathing. Ambition.

It would be beyond midnight. She got up, restless, and went to the bathroom and then paced her bedroom. She picked up the souvenir snow globe and she shook white confusion all over the plastic cutout skyline of Manhattan, then set the paperweight down again. At the window she peered out. Nothing was changed. Nothing changed in New York City except of course that everything changed a thousand times faster than one could ever notice.

Later, as she was almost asleep, she wondered if an angel had entered her room. But any angels she knew about, like angels in stained glass windows or angels in the Italian Renaissance rooms of the Met, those guys never arrived at night. They needed full light to be pictured. Angels at night were invisible. There was nothing there. Perhaps Laura wasn't really there either.

No one stood nearby to look down at the girl in the bed and witness whether or not she really existed.

8

Monday morning broke with the anarchy of a school holiday but without the privilege of relief. By 7:45 A.M., everyone else she knew was already in homeroom. It was the last school day before the break. Laura wasn't supposed to show up and clear out her locker and hand in her textbooks until after release at three. Fewer goodbyes, less chance of guerrilla ambush in the corridors of war. Maxine Sugargarten and Donna Flotarde and Doll Pettigrew and the others would have to strut along and seize upon some other victim. Happy holidays to *that* sucker.

She dressed and went downstairs. In the front hall she found Nonno in his store whites. He was holding the door open for the repair fellows, that John Greenglass, that Sam-the-helper, who brought in a cardboard box of supplies and tool belts.

"It no working," Nonno was saying to them. "Is no good. You no find hole. Look, such disaster. *Mia moglie,* she have nervous screaming from this." The ceiling was damper than before. It looked nasty.

"We did some caulking on Saturday but we must not have got it all," said John. "I promise you, Mr. Ovid, we'll seal it up good. More snow isn't called for till later. By the time you get home tonight the breach will be plugged. The walls and ceiling will take a day or two to dry out, and we can do a quick paint job on Wednesday. Our level best, that's all we can give."

Sam scowled at the ceiling. "Any more owls show up?"

Signore Ciardi hadn't heard about the owl but he didn't bother to ask Sam what the hell he was talking about. "You look in bedroom. See if is worse in there, too. Signora go out this morning. She leaving soon." Laura knew he meant: So the busybody old lady won't be in your way with her hand-wringing and suchlike.

He saw her on the stairs. "Laura. Don't bother men. What you doing here?"

"I'm not allowed to go to school today, Nonno. *Again.* Remember?"

"*Abbi pietà, o Signore.* Well, take breakfast, stay out

of sight. Workers they finish today or Nonna she serve my head on platter for Christmas Eve buffet."

"How is the owl?" Laura asked Sam.

"I'm not making funnies, Laura. *Vai fuori di qui.*" Nonno was old-fashioned and didn't like Laura to speak to men.

"The little white owl is home," replied Sam. "My mama is feeding her pellets of raw hamburger. Don't think she's strong enough to fly out into this snowstorm yet. When the weather clears and she's better, I gonna release her in Central Park."

"Does she have a name?"

"Laura!" said Nonno, pulling his unfastened bow tie at both ends, as if getting ready to wrap it around her neck.

"We call her Fluster," said Sam. Laura grinned and fled to the kitchen.

Mary Bernice was in a cheery mood. She was making a shopping list for the Christmas Eve dinner. Eventually Nonna would descend to the kitchen like a queen and wrap an apron on her big bosom and do most of the cooking herself, because she didn't trust an Irishwoman to do convincing Neapolitan dishes. But the supplies had to be ready. The onions and garlic, the several sorts of fish, the tomatoes and herbs. Anything precious and packaged would come from Ciardi's counters and shelves, but a lot of the list was standard supermarket fare. "The lads are back to have another go at the drip drip drip, I hear," said Mary Bernice to Laura. "Rosa Mendoza is in those Honduras, don't you know, so I was going to start this morning in the parlor and maneuver the Hoover. But it's scarcely worth it, what with the workers tramping about. Now, will you join me going round to the shops and help me carry things home?"

"Do I have to?"

"Anyone you want to avoid will be in school, so why not?"

"Their mothers."

"Ah, the parade of mothers. I see. Well, I can manage on my own sure enough, don't I do so every week. But I thought you might like a distraction."

"I have to think about packing for prison. I have to lay all my clothes out on the bed and see if anything needs mending."

"All righty-o, but I'm going to nab you when I get back. With Mrs. Ciardi's sister and her fella coming this year, the fuss has gone feverish. You best stay upstairs and out of the way of those two handsome johnnies, now."

"I'm not allowed to talk to anyone," said Laura blankly. "Anyone. Ever."

"Right, and you've done such a good job so far obeying every instruction that you're being sent out of the country," said Mary Bernice, without malice or mockery. "Mind your p's and q's, young Laura."

As she ate her Maypo, Laura listened to the little domestic fanfare of departures. When the coast was clear, she tiptoed up to the front hall. The drop cloths were down and the stepladders opened. Sam and John must be upstairs somewhere. Laura climbed to the second floor and peered into the parlor, then the third and checked out her grandparents' bedroom. The noises were still higher. Well, no one told me I couldn't go back to my own bedroom, she thought, so she followed Garibaldi as he sped his way to the attic level.

Cold air was rushing in the open window of the box room. John and Sam had already pried off the lid of a plastic tub of some kind of purplish gunk. They readied a paint tray and some trowels for application outside. "There she is, fresh from the winter season at Cape Canaveral," said John when Laura appeared at the door. To her inquiry, he said, "First we have to check and see if what we slapped on the other day has gapped, leaving a channel for more snowmelt to get in. If so, we'll plug it with more grouting compound and trim the excess. Then I'm going to get up the slope of the mansard and double-check the seals just below the parapet. We finished them already, but water's still getting in somewhere."

"That sounds dangerous. Can I help?"

"Sam will spot me. You can stay out of the way." Perhaps that sounded meaner than John had intended, but Laura took it as a rejection, and she sidled into her room. She didn't close the door. She could hear the guys next door. She could tell when John was sitting on the windowsill and inching out. He must be putting his weight on a narrow ledge, a stone gutter built into the wall below the mansard windows on the top flight. It was just wide enough for a male foot set sideways.

The arc of losing one's balance, veering backward, falling: the tragic parabolic swoop. Feeling the plummet in the pit of her stomach, Laura nearly gave up her breakfast, but was able to recover. She took solace in folding the ribbed sleeves of her white school sweaters into neat cross-the-breast X's. One, two, three, and there was a fourth somewhere, maybe at the dry cleaner's.

The girl knew nothing about Montreal except that it was north. Whatever cold and snow could fall in Manhattan would likely be doubled up there. In a way, it is hard to fear a change when you can't even picture it. All she could do was

imagine that she might come to dread a new place, too. This slow folding of sweaters was a delay. No help in the long run.

As if thinking about falling had made it come to pass, she heard a terrible sound, a thump, and an inarticulate wordless yelp. Sam shouted something. Laura ran into the box room. Sam was leaning out the window. Gripping Sam's forearms, John was dangling above Van Pruyn Place.

He wasn't speaking, John; he was saving his breath. Sam called over his shoulder into the room. "Laura. That rope! Quick now." She scooped up the coiled length and joined Sam at the window. "Make a loop and let it out. John can slip his other foot in it." She did as she was told, but her hands trembled. She wasn't trying to save John from dying, only to save his foot. How calm these guys were. As if they fell off rooftops every week.

She wrapped most of the rope around her waist but dropped out a segment the way Sam suggested. "It's not open enough," grunted Sam. "Lean out and divide the sides so he can get his foot in." Laura was afraid of being dragged out, but she managed to part the sides of the dropped noose till it was nearly a foot wide, and she caught John's madly circling left foot.

Now she could see that his right foot was already lodged in the gutter, but it was at an awkward angle from which he couldn't right himself on his own. His center of gravity was too low. "Walk it backward, bring it up," said Sam.

Laura retreated into the box room, her waist and her hands pulling on the rope. John's foot rose with it up to the level of the ledge. He was able to hook his second foot over the parapet, but his body sagged, and his rump cantilevered out into the wind. Still, now that he had some purchase, and with Sam tugging with panicky might, John pushed with his calves and elevated his torso so his head was partway in the window. Then Laura could grab him under one armpit, and in a blur of energy, by instinct more than design, they managed together to haul John in the window. They fell into a heap of limbs and rope and scattered snow on the floorboards, and lay there panting.

Laura turned her head. John's eyes were closed; he was breathing himself to safety. On John's other side, Sam had raised himself to an elbow. He was looking at her.

"You did it," she said. "You rescued him."

"We did it," he told her. "Good job. Can you make us a pot of tea while we pull ourselves together and see if we can keep going here?"

"Milk and sugar," said John from behind his closed eyelids.

By the time she came back upstairs, feeling like Mary Bernice with a tray of tea things and some imported nougat, the lads were already back at work. John was outside again, this time with a safety rope tied around his waist. Sam was passing supplies back. They'd gone through half a bucket of that gunk already. Laura felt incidental and useless. She set the tea down without comment, and left the room.

The way men fall.

But there was nothing more to say about that. She went back to cotton percale shirts. She decided not to start on her Playtex and nylons and garter belts until after the men had finished upstairs.

Sometime later—she'd lost track of the time—John Greenglass paused in her doorway. He had the rope around his shoulder and the empty bucket in one meaty hand. "You saved my life today," said John. "Merry Christmas to you." Behind his shoulder, Sam winked at her.

"And a happy new year to you," she said, stupidly. Because what else was there to say? You're welcome?

"Your grandmother will be happy. We found the problem and I think we fixed it," said John. "Just in time, too, because a new cold front is slamming down the coast—fierce wind and snow from the maritimes expected by midnight."

"Oh."

"Thanks for the tea," said Sam. "I'll bring this kitchen stuff downstairs. You did a good job with that rope, Laura Ciardi. Couldna done it without you."

She looked at the shiny white toes of her saddle shoes. "Everybody has to rescue themselves," she said, sounding like Miss Parsley.

"Not us, we rescue each other," said Sam.

"Uh-huh," said John, and thumped away heavily, as if so happy to be alive that he didn't mind if he broke every step in the attic staircase. Sam grinned and pretended to kick John in the rear end as he followed him down the stairs. Sam, Sam. Sam Rescue, that would be his name, as long as Laura didn't know what his real last name might be.

9

At about two-thirty that afternoon Laura poked her head in the parlor door. Nonna was sitting and making notes with a Bic pen. She seemed surprised to see Laura, as if she thought Laura would already have taken herself off to Montreal. "I got so involved," she said. "The Sodality is doing the coffee hour after High Mass on Christmas morning and Mrs. Pill is going to be out in Hicksville with her daughter's family, so it has fallen to me. Why are you so dressed up? You're not thinking of going out."

"You remember? I have to clear out my locker and hand in my books? Also I'm doing my last hour with the after-school first graders."

"Laurita, I've been thinking about that. Maybe you'd

better not tell the *bambinos* you won't be back after the Christmas break."

"Why not?"

"Do you think it would be kind? Small children form attachments."

"Are they the only ones who do?" asked Laura flatly. She thought it would be nastier just to disappear without warning, but maybe Nonna was right. Maybe with the delights of Christmas, her kids wouldn't even notice when she didn't show up again in January. "Well, Mr. G. said I was to see out my term on this, and it's the last day today. So I'm going to school. But I'll wait at the counter at Moxie's until everyone gets dismissed. I don't feel like bumping into anybody."

Nonna put her pen to her lips and looked at her granddaughter without speaking for a moment. Then she laid the ballpoint down and said levelly, "Would you like me to come with you, Laura?"

Almost the weirdest thing the old lady had ever said. But probably it was meant kindly. "No," said Laura, then, "I mean: no, thank you."

"Well," said Nonna. "It won't be fun, but what has fun got to do with it? We'll expect you back, what, about four-thirty?"

"More or less." Laura shrugged and headed out without saying goodbye.

In the front hall, John Greenglass was perched near the top of the stepladder. He was checking some measurements with a collapsible wooden yardstick fitted with brass hinges. "Think we've got it," he told Laura. "The drip is yesterday's news. We're cutting the plasterboard to install it tomorrow, assuming the ceiling can finish drying out overnight."

"No more owls," said Laura.

"One owl is weird enough. More would be haunted."

"You going out, we see you tomorrow," said Sam. He winked at her again. He had a gold tooth about halfway back that glinted when he grinned, and the glint brought rose and copper into his soft brown face. "I'll tell Fluster you said hi."

The street was scraped by wind and torn branches. The little New York city trees pinched between sidewalks and curbs, all adolescent, were half buried in shoveled snow. It was a wonder they could make it through the winter.

She didn't need to stop at Moxie's because the kids were already coursing out the doors of Driscoll, fifteen minutes early. Mr. G. must have been full of Christmas cheer. When the surge had spent itself, Laura took a deep breath and pushed in the front door. A school could go from full to empty in three minutes flat. The silence echoing in the corridors made Laura feel a thousand years older than fifteen. She grabbed a few things from her locker and dropped her schoolbooks on a bench for someone in charge to find them.

Then holiday music jingle-belled itself over the loudspeaker, and a burst of adult hilarity rolled from the front offices. Maybe the teachers were having a glass of eggnog before heading off for their own vacations. Laura went the other way to Staircase B—the crime scene—and climbed up two flights. The library door was open and the lights were on, but half the work desks were crowded to one side of the room. The librarian, Mr. Xaridopoulos, was stacking chairs on top of the study table. "Hi, Mr. X.," said Laura in a small voice, and said it again because he didn't hear her, what with chair-leg banging and scraping.

"Oh, you," he said. "Looking for a book to read to your little kids? They're not coming *here* today." He gestured. Tarps over most of the dictionaries and the picture book section. "Broken pipes upstairs. You can grab something from the fairy tales if you can reach them. I'm locking up in two minutes."

"But the little kids. Where are they?"

"Cafeteria. I think the cook is going to make them hot chocolate. They can't come in here, it's a disaster area."

Librarians love nothing better than a disaster because then they can prove they are the rescuers of civilization they are so sure already that they are.

She grabbed a volume of Hans Christian Andersen stories. The pictures were insipid, wreathed in daisies and crawling with ladybugs, but by experience Laura knew the stories to be strong enough to hold a small population of displaced first graders. "Have a nice Christmas, Mr. X.," she said. He chortled noncommittally.

The cafeteria smelled of corned beef and stale sneakers. The janitor was already mopping the floor with dirty sudsy water. He looked as if he were adding a layer of filth instead of erasing it. "Are we meeting in here?" asked Laura, as bravely as she could.

The janitor replied, "There you are, and here am I, and the moon's in the sky and a song in my heart. Would you move your foot, thank you."

"The first-grade after-school kids? Because the library's closed due to the pipes?"

The kids were clattering downstairs now, arrived from Driscoll Primary around the corner. "So it seems," said the janitor, and gave up trying to correct his little universe with a mop. "Santa's elves in a frenzy. And so the nightmare continues."

The chaperone, Miss Gerstein, came in with the last small child. Miss Gerstein was rattled. "Up the stairs and down the stairs! And pipes bursting in both buildings, did you hear? Laura, can you manage storytime? I have to run pick up a prescription for my mother, who is having angina attacks on the hour."

Laura was used to this. Actually she preferred it when Miss Gerstein stole time for personal errands. She just waved Miss G. out the door and opened the book.

"I hope it's Christmas story time," said Bernard.

"But not Baby Jesus. I hate Baby Jesus. I'm Jewish," said Rita.

"Some Christmas party," said Mugsy. "Feels like torture."

"They said hot chocolate," said Xian Lee. "Milk makes me sick but I *love* it."

"Shhh," said Laura, and opened the book. She knew the twelve stories in this collection, and had read most of them already. Not "The Ugly Duckling," not "The Steadfast Tin Soldier." Not "The Emperor's New Clothes," even though the kids loved nakedness of any variety. Not "The Little Mermaid"; it was too long, and so was "The Snow Queen." "The Little Match

Girl" was too sad. Laura settled on the final story in the book, which she had read to herself last September when she'd first been asked to help out at the afterschool program. It was called "The Wild Swans." Like a lot of the Andersen stories, it rambled. The dozen or so kids were in no mood for rambling stories, but they needed something to settle them, especially here in the creepy basement cafeteria instead of the cozy library they were used to.

"Okay," said Laura, "everybody sit in this corner. Sit on your coats because the floor is cold."

"It's wet," said Mugsy. "That guy mopped here. Yuck. It stinks like I don't know what."

It did stink, and Laura knew of what, but she didn't say.

Christmas fever. It was going to be hard to hold them. Though Laura could read to young kids in a way she couldn't even read to herself, this afternoon the prose failed to command their attention. So she slammed the book closed with a bang. This shut the kids up and made them straighten their spines, and two of them put their thumbs in their mouths. "I'm just going to tell you this story. It'll go faster. When we're done we can march around the tables."

"March *on* the tables," suggested Bernard. But they quieted down.

Laura made quick work of the story. There was a girl with eleven big brothers. When their father married a wicked Queen, the new wife tired of the noisy boys and turned them into swans. One by one they flew out the window into the wide wide world. The girl alone was left to do all the work.

The little girls were nodding, and the boys were nodding, too. So far so good.

Laura told how the swan-brothers came back to see their sister once a year and how they turned back into her brothers for one hour, but they always became swans again at the stroke of midnight on New Year's Eve and flew away.

"My aunt had a stroke," said Fiona. "I think it was a stroke of midnight because she was lying on the floor until after breakfast-time."

The girl searched for ways to rescue her brothers but had no luck until finally (how did this go again?) she met someone, maybe a good witch, who told her to weave eleven cambric shirts out of the thread of moonlight. Next New Year's Eve, when they turned into swans at the stroke of midnight, she should throw an enchanted shirt over each swan. They would turn back into her brothers and the spell would be lifted for good.

"Well, that's convenient," said Leonora. "Still, more work for her. Figures."

"Swans can't make shirts, they gots no hands," said Philbert. "They should just get a gun and shoot the old Queen."

So the girl found out how to spin moonlight into thread, or something like that, and weave thread into fabric, and she worked day and night for eleven months of the year. On New Year's Eve, all the swans flew in her window after bedtime, so the Queen and the King wouldn't know. They became her brothers again for one hour. The sister had the eleven shirts ready. When the clock started striking twelve and her brothers turned back into swans, she tossed one shirt after another over them. They changed back into her brothers for good and hugged her and said thanks a lot. Except for the youngest brother, her favorite. His shirt wasn't done. The final sleeve wasn't finished. When she threw the shirt over his noble swan body, he turned back into her favorite brother, except for one arm, which remained a swan wing.

"Then they all went and shot the Queen. Merry Christmas and happy new year!" shouted Philbert.

The hot chocolate came. Miss Gerstein came back. The janitor said they had to leave the cafeteria because he needed to keep swabbing the deck. Miss Gerstein led the children up Staircase B, hunting for someplace else to spend the last half hour of after-school. At the landing with the emergency exit out to the alley next to the school, Laura set the Andersen stories down, opened the door, and slipped out. Snow was blowing. An alarm began to ring but gave up after a lackluster pipping. No one noticed her departure. She sidled down the alley between some wooden pallets stored on their side and a broken red Coke dispensary machine, and she became anonymous again in New York City.

10

Mary Bernice said, “They expect you to sit down with them and have a bite of supper. They want to hear how your afternoon went.”

Laura scowled. “Can you tell them I have a headache?”

This was code for you-know-what, but Mary Bernice replied, “Go up and join them. I’m not covering for you this time. I have the chicken cacciatore to plate while you’re enjoying them scraps of rabbit food they call salad.”

So Laura went up. The dining room was set for three, as usual. On weekdays Mary Bernice removed the fussy lace tablecloth and she set out hard place mats with scenes from sunny Italy painted on them. The Leaning Tower of Pisa, the canals of Venice, Saint Peter's in Rome. Today Laura got the Coliseum. "I'm working out the seating plan for Christmas Eve," said Nonna. "I want to know who you would like to sit next to."

This was her way of being nice—really she didn't care what Laura would like. Or where she sat. Laura said, "Can't I eat in the dungeon with Mary Bernice?"

"Grace," declared Nonno, and led the prayer. A caesura, a daily truce lasting twelve seconds.

Then Nonna said, "No, you can't eat in the kitchen. My sister hasn't seen you in many years, and Christmas is for families, Laura. So we have Nonno at the head of the table like the prince he is, and I will sit at the foot. Zia Geneva will sit at Nonno's right and Mr. Corm Kennedy at mine. That leaves four other places. One for you, one for Mr. Vincequerra from the store—his wife is suddenly in Bellevue, don't ask why—and one each for the Polumbos. The stout Polumbos from the nine o'clock Mass, not the thin Polumbos from the noon. Who do you want to sit next to?"

Laura didn't care about this tonight. "Oh, Nonno, I guess."

"Laura," said Nonno, "you got friend you want come? We got room for more chairs." He gestured with his fork. The table could take up to three leaves without crowding the sideboard. It was a good-size room with wallpaper showing Italian shepherds and milkmaids dancing in a rustic lane. From the beamed ceiling a chandelier dripped with teardrop crystal prisms. The effect was bright but ragged, because some of the pendants were missing.

If Laura were to admit aloud that at this point her only friends were the first graders in the after-school program, Nonno's face would just go slatted with worry. She thought to say, "Everyone I know will be with their own families."

"*Sì,* that's normal." He shrugged, smiled; problem solved.

"Will you ask my mother to come?"

She regretted the words the instant they sounded in the room. Nonno set his fork down so softly it didn't make a sound. He removed his napkin from the collar of his shirt. He dabbed his mouth with a peculiar daintiness. "She no come, Laurita, she no come, you no ask for this." His voice was hard, angry, offended maybe.

"You're going back to the docks, Vito," said Nonna, which was her way to chastise him into remembering his Better English. His accent tended to backslide when he was upset. "Laura, this isn't the time to be in touch. It isn't a good time for your mother."

"It's never a good time for *her,*" said Laura.

"Not good time for *us*," said Nonno, which wasn't Laura's point, but she felt herself becoming a little shaky. She put both hands in her lap and twisted her fingers together.

There was a girl at Christmastime whose mother never—

But that wasn't even a full sentence, and she couldn't think through the idea, because, oh, too vast, too vast, the number of things that the *mother never.*

No father—some mishap in the U.S. occupation of Austria had killed him a few months before Laura was born. No brother—claimed by an accident a decade later, but just as lost—and no mother, because she had chosen to evaporate, go upstate, leaving Laura with her Ciardi grandparents. The original Thing One and Thing Two grown huge and ancient. Were they monstrous and selfish, or only clueless?

"The truth about your mother is—" began Nonna.

"*Carissima,*" interrupted Nonno, leveling a hand, palm down, signaling. Cut it out. Not now. You mean well but for the love of Christ, shut up.

"She should be *facing* this, Ovid," replied Nonna. "She has a right to know."

"Nobody talk nonsense about Renata, she so sick.

Leave her be. And don't talk across Laurita as if she deaf. She no deaf and she no stupid."

Nonna raised an eyebrow. She probably meant, Neither am I, Ovid; give me some credit. But Laura felt stung. She said, as much to change the subject for herself as for her grandparents, "Well, if not Mama, what about John Greenglass? Or the other guy? Or both of them?"

"Don't be silly, you're being silly, don't," said Nonna, but her voice was back to its normal register, part kindly and part fed up.

"They got their own families, and they're just worker *cretini* anyway," said Nonno. He leaned forward, a bit relieved to have left the subject of Renata Ciardi aside. "Is time for talking about boy thing, *tesoro mio*? No? Maybe so. Your nonna sit you down after supper and give you lesson."

"Ovid Ciardi, you've lost your mind," said Nonna. "It's no such time and I'll make no such lesson plan. Laura is going to a convent school in two weeks. Not a moment too soon it seems. Laura, mind yourself. I feel a migraine in the roots of my hair. Nonno meant you could invite a girlfriend from school, but he was just being polite to you because he loves you, you fool." How tenderly she could say *fool,* it was the way other people said *lover*—or so Laura imagined.

"We keep you safe year after year, we keep you safe still!" shouted Nonno, and knocked over his glass of wine. His voice was full of some kind of fierce triumph. She was probably supposed to say thank you, but she knew her expression betrayed her thought: *Safe from what?*

Mary Bernice came in and mopped up the wine. She had been waiting in the pantry to take the main course out of the dumbwaiter and bring it through. "Shall I clear this rubbish, then," she said, which was dismissive of her own cooking, but Laura saw the jest in it. Mary Bernice brought Laura a glass of Chianti mixed with Coca-Cola. Laura wondered if the nuns of Montreal would serve this for dinner, too.

Over the figs and nuts, Nonna carried on about the fat Polumbos, about the Vincequerra marriage, about Mr. Corm Kennedy and how he had swept Geneva Bentivengo Mastrangelo off her elderly ankles after her first husband died. "You'll be between Nonno and Mr. Vincequerra," said Nonna decisively. "He's very nice and you will ask him about anything except why his wife has gone to a lunatic ward. Though if he tells you why, remember every word. I want to know."

"I think we should at least invite my mother," said Laura. "Who cares about these others? If she's sick, all the more reason to ask her to come visit."

"You know nothing," snapped Nonna. "Go to your room, you ungrateful goat."

"You every reason we have to live," said Nonno, getting up and bowing formally to his granddaughter, but his face was *pomodoro.*

Then why are you sending me away, Laura wanted to know. They were demented, that's why. She threw her napkin on her plate and fled up the stairs to her safe garret. The storm had begun again. The skylight at the top of the stairwell was an iron lid of frozen snow. Her room was a prison, a treehouse morgue.

She lay on her bed in the cold room, in the dark, and began to die.

11

What was wind, was it a pushing or a resisting, or was it both.

Pushing and resisting, motion and rest. Waking and sleeping, living and drowning.

No tell left in her. The efforts at narration, only sputtery abortions.

There was

and

It must

but they didn't tinder up enough to flame a single sentence. The push too weak, the resistance too powerful.

She was listening for nothing. Though she caught Mary Bernice singsong her goodbyes from below.

Later, Laura heard Nonna laboring upstairs to follow Nonno to bed on the third floor. In the hall at the base of the steep flight to the attic, Nonna was pausing to catch her breath. "Laura, Laurita, Laura," called Nonna, though a few minutes later Laura wondered if that had been Nonna or the wind. The gale whipping in from Long Island Sound was a ventriloquist.

In any case, Laura did not answer with a whispered *what?* until after their bedroom door had closed and the sound of the toilet flushing offered legitimate cover. And Nonno's album of the nightly opera began to spin its overtures and arias and choruses through the floorboards. Mary Bernice thought it scandalous that people so old should have a hi-fi in their bedroom; it somehow didn't seem at all proper and certainly not Catholic. Sometimes the cook had wondered aloud about her employers. So venal, so pagan.

Tonight it was *Tancredi. "L'aura che intorno spiri . . ."* The very air you breathe brings mortal threat, if Nonno's translations on Laura's behalf were to be trusted. If her own memory was to be trusted. The beginning was filled with urgent high notes that sound like someone signaling a whole fleet of taxis. Maybe Nonno intended this nightly musical interlude to be a lullaby kiss for

Laura, since at this point neither he nor his wife could make it up that final flight of steps. In any case, Laura had learned to tune out the private broadcast. Tonight the melodramas of Rossini were little more than aural wash, subsumed by the roar of tidal winds. Gale force, Atlantic arias in *accelerando* and *fortissimo.* Laura almost felt seasick, as if the building were veering.

The music ended and the toilet below flushed again, and the house hunched on its mighty limestone thighs, holding tight against the assault of the storm. Through her closed eyes Laura saw snowflakes as if from grave eternity, spinning through the cold and lonely universe with no place to land. Particles of white nothing, with nothing to adhere to. Storybooks torn into scraps so small not a single whole word survived, just the orphaned alphabet.

She felt a sudden aggressive thump in her spine and forearms, and in the very frame of the bed, too, or so it seemed. She sat up and opened her eyes. Nonna had fallen out of bed, must be; or Nonno had tumbled over that ridiculous ottoman in the corner. But had one of them gotten hurt, the other would be hollering. There was no sound of panic from below except a single exploratory complaint from Garibaldi, who stalked the halls at nighttime and sometimes ended up on Laura's bed by dawn, if she left her door open.

She got out of the bed and stood quite still in her cotton flannel nightgown with the drippy red rosebuds and the blue ink stain on the sleeve from that time she had fallen asleep doing homework in bed. The floor was ice. The radiators began to hiss and clank like a factory in thrombosis, in overdrive.

"What is it," she said, though whether aloud or to herself she didn't know.

Oh goody, I'm having a nervous breakdown, she said to herself. She felt a little giddy, because those were words she never had quite understood. A higher-class sort of diagnosis. People in Nonna's Sodality were always having nervous breakdowns; it seemed quite the thing. Nonna thought it was all complete and utter *cavolo,* but sometimes she spoke of it as if she wished she could try it, too, not unlike wanting to go to Elizabeth Arden someday before she died.

Another sound, not a thump but more of a scrabbling and maybe a moan. Not in Van Pruyn Place and not downstairs, but outside— Outside her window—

She was afraid to look. There was no way an intruder could climb up the outside of the building from the street level, not without a fireman's extendable ladder. But the sound. Could one of those slender curbside baby trees have been uprooted and catapulted aloft by the winds to catch in the high stone gutter?

Baby trees don't generally moan, unless they did so during your own personal private nervous breakdown.

Laura had never gone downstairs to knock on her grandparents' bedroom door during the night. Once or twice, in the grip of the throwups, Laura had presented herself to Miss Gianna Tebaldi in her room down the hall from Laura's. But it had been years since the governess had gotten pregnant and run off with the RCA repairman. So the house was bereft of useful backup, what with Nonno already snoring so hard that Nonna probably had her earplugs in.

The noise was becoming a scrabbling that sounded less furtive than desperate. What worse could happen to me, thought Laura. Leaving her light off, she inched up to the window. She stayed close to the wall so she couldn't be seen. She was in The Twilight Zone Hotel. She peered into the flatness of a hard close snow. She thought she saw a rack of ice raking up and down.

It's the mother, it's the white owl's mother, and it's coming looking for Fluster, she thought. But what a mother—it must be as big as I am.

A wounded animal was less frightening than a prowler or a rapist. Laura hurried to the box room next door. The creature had landed against the roof closer to the box room window. Maybe she could keep the creature from blowing away again, or falling to its death.

She opened the lower half of the sash as high as she could get it. Since John Greenglass had been in and out that morning, the window was only a little stuck with snow and ice. She leaned into the storm.

She had seen this already today. She must be dreaming it again. But even in a dream every attempt must be made. She scurried backward, grabbed the coil of rope as she had that morning. Looping it double, she ducked her head and shoulders out into the storm again. Instantly drenched with icy snow, she managed to secure the flailing foot. It was naked, and blue in the stormlight. "Bloody eejit, get in here, you, before you catch your death," she said, an homage to Mary Bernice Molloy, late of County Tyrone and currently residing in Brooklyn.

The castaway in the high winds wasn't as much in danger of falling as John Greenglass had been. He was splayed across the imbricated tiles of the insloping mansard roof, held there by the flat hand of the wind. Laura pulled at his looped foot. To keep his balance, he had no choice but to inch toward the window. When both his thighs were in front of the window—he was trousered in some coarse blue buckram—she said, "Now you'll lean sideways and get your shoulders in from the cold, and the rest will be easy as a piece of pizza pie."

Whether he was obeying her or just following his own instincts for survival, she didn't know. One way or the other he got his drenched head in—a shaggy head of wildly unshorn and dirty-straw hair, more curled wood shavings than anything else. Then his navy tunic-ed torso, then the knees and bare frozen feet. One arm reached out for Laura and she took it boldly if formally, square at the forearm, just as she might the arm of some elderly gentleman struggling to get out of a pew. The castaway toppled in at an angle and his other arm was last, flexing in a complicated sequence of compression as he slowly straightened his spine; only it wasn't an arm at all, and why should she be surprised, so she wasn't, not after finding a young man blown onto her roof: the other arm swept in, a vast snowy wing of a swan.

12

He straightened up but his eyes were trained on the floor. He was taller than she was by half a head. The wing trembled and shook out wetness in what seemed an involuntary motion. He turned his head the other way and ducked his chin to his shoulder. When the wing had settled again, he managed to raise his eyes to look at her. His eyes were heavy-lidded like those of some sorry-lot ladies Laura had seen over toward Times Square after a matinee of *My Fair Lady* last year. Before she could finish the thought, though, his knees seemed to buckle and he thudded to the floor of the box room.

That's my effect on boys, right there, Laura thought.

She stood in turmoil, twisting her hands together as if a classic and clueless bystander. But when she heard the door open downstairs and Nonno's ratchety voice called up to her to see if she was all right, she was levelheaded enough to reply, "I'm sorry for waking you, Nonno. I dropped something."

"Go to bed and stop dropping things, *e buonanotte e sogni d'oro,*" he advised, and closed the door behind him.

The visitor's eyes had closed. A vicious-smelling dribble had slanted a question-mark on the floor. Laura ran into her bathroom and grabbed a towel, and then ducked into her bedroom for her comforter and the chenille spread. She put on the lamp next to her bed to provide some indirect lighting. Returning to the box room, she mopped up the vomit beside the creature. Creature? Man? Boy? Bird? Boy seemed nearest. It wasn't quite accurate. It would have to do. The boy's breathing settled almost at once. He curled onto his arm side, fetally, and the wing came forward like a sheet. Had he been naked underneath it, he'd still be modest. She flapped her bedclothes over him. He seemed not to notice. Whatever else he was or wasn't, he was exhausted. He was going to revive or going to die, but either way he was going to do it privately under his wing, under her blankets.

For a few moments she crouched in the doorway,

ready to spring up and flee if he should rouse and get aggressive. When Garibaldi came padding by and rubbed against her hip, she almost fell over—his suddenness felt more startling than the arrival of a half-winged boy. The cat was halfway to a purr, but at the sight of the intruder Garibaldi began to hiss. Laura swatted him away and closed the door of the box room.

Without forming clear plans, she found herself tiptoeing downstairs. This wasn't so unusual; sometimes she went down and got some Life cereal in the middle of the night if she was hungry. Garibaldi came with her, head down and irritated but probably hoping for some milk out of the campaign. Which he got.

She took one of the trays on which Mary Bernice piled meals for the dumbwaiter. Since the apparatus didn't rise all the way to the attic Laura prepared to carry the tray up herself. She set out some bread and some cold lasagne in extra sauce, some imported artichoke hearts in oil and red and green peppercorns, a glass of milk, and then, making a quick act of contrition in case it was a sin, a juice glass filled with a nice Montepulciano. Silverware, and two paper napkins in case he was a sloppy eater. That should do it.

Before she left, she refilled Garibaldi's saucer with milk. This kept the cat engaged while she closed the door behind him. No more feline bother for this evening.

Back upstairs, she set the tray down on the floor of the box room. Feeling cold herself, she ventured back into the room that Miss Gianna Tebaldi had once occupied. The bed had been taken out and given to the Salvation Army, but after all these years the blankets and pillows were still folded up on the dresser. She took an armful of everything and returned to the box room. Now that the cat was secured in the kitchen, she could leave the door open. She made herself a pallet, with her feet in her own room and her head on a pillow in the hall, facing the box room door. She was at the same level as her guest. All she could see were his naked feet and the mound of covers gently rising and falling, proof he had not yet died.

His feet. One was lateral to the floor. The other foot lay atop it but cantilevered toward her, so she could examine the sole of the forward foot minutely. If there was a practice to telling fortunes by reading the soles of feet instead of the palms of hands, she could get to work and tell his fortune. But she couldn't even tell if he was human. She just looked at the feet as if they were an art project she was supposed to be drawing.

What can you tell of a boy by his feet? They were hard and callused at the toes, especially the back ridges of the four smaller toes. Stony, as if frostbit. The tender inward-arching sole was gammon pink, and surely that was a sign of a functioning circulatory system. (Thank you, Miss Frobisher.) The ball of the top foot, the one she could see better, had a blooded scar, but the cut wasn't deep. The foot looked clammy with melting snow from the cuffs of the rough trousers and the ice-crud that might have formed between his toes.

Then she began to worry about the toes falling off—how embarrassing that would be!—and she remembered Christ washing the feet of the sinner with oil. What the hell. She retrieved the dish of artichokes and poured some oil in her hands, sieving out the peppercorns. Wincing with uncertainty—she didn't want to hurt him, for the love of all the saints and angels!—she put her hands upon his feet and massaged softly.

He didn't flinch, he didn't kick in shock. When she was done she reached for the towel and held it along his feet to absorb the moisture. As long as he was still fast asleep or playing dead, she grew bolder and rubbed his feet harder. It only took a moment. When she was done, his toes looked more orange than white. She hoped she hadn't accelerated their detaching, but she decided the color was from increased blood flow.

Setting aside the towel again, she put her head back on her pillow. Two feet from his own two feet, she watched him for some indefinite length of midnight. The green light upcast from the hall below began to waver. In the way of sleep, she was waking again in somewhat brighter light before she was certain she could ever fall asleep again.

13

But either it wasn't a dream after all or she had really better make a reservation at the funny farm, because she woke up on the floor of the attic hallway. The snow hadn't stopped falling, but it had grown thinner. You could see through it to the top windows and carved rooflines of the brownstones across Van Pruyn Place. The wind had dropped some, too, now just a workaday bluster. The house was silent. It was about dawn. Christmas Eve was coming, Christmas Day. Unless the storm had slowed the subways or choked the streets, Mary Bernice would be here soon to start breakfast for the grandparents. John Greenglass and Sam Who-Could-He-Be—oh, Sam Rescue, that's right—would arrive to finish the repair of the front hall ceiling.

She sat up slowly. The chenille bedspread, her bedspread, was on the floor in the box room. The room was empty. The window was closed. Her comforter wasn't on the floor or in her bedroom.

Menace, danger, worry, holiday eggnog with strychnine. What a menu.

She hopped to the bathroom because the floor was icy, and closed the door behind her. Then she locked it, something she had never done before. She used the toilet and washed her hands and scrubbed her teeth with a dry toothbrush, just to wake herself up. Her hairbrush was in the bedroom, but she soothed and smoothed her hair as best she could with her hands.

She found him crouching in a stain of brightness in a corner of Miss Gianna Tebaldi's old room. (Oh he was still here he was still here he was still here.)

He must have stepped over her while she slept. The coverlet was up to his chin and his eyes were closed. The tray she had brought up—the milk was gone, and also the wine. The lasagne, sagging laterally, looked disagreeable, and she didn't wonder that he had left it. Maybe he couldn't work a fork? For the first time she stopped to figure out which arm he had, and which wing. She wasn't good at left and right in the best of times, and even worse at working out someone else's left and right. But she stood there and took her time. The left wing, the right arm. So unless he was left-handed he could probably use a fork. But fork and knife at once, no. She ought to have thought of that. She ought to have cut the slab of cold lasagne for him. It looked viciously unappealing in the daylight.

He was asleep, or he was in a coma. He wasn't dead, for his shoulders rose and fell with the work of his lungs.

Not knowing what to do, how even to think about what this was all about, she stood there and stared at the crown of curls that had dried into crisp, clotted circlets of pale beach sand. Maybe salt water had clumped the ringlets together. At the Jersey shore, when people came out of the water and fell asleep in the sun, sometimes their hair went stiff like that. Like a natural perm.

She tried to tell it to herself so she could understand it better. But.

. . . . . . !

Not a word came to her head. The storyteller inside her was defeated by the irruption of real story.

She could see him. How could this be real? But it couldn't be a dream. None of the walls were sliding about. Time wasn't slippery. Details that she didn't need to notice were there, regardless. The moccasins that Miss Gianna Tebaldi had bought in *LAKE GEORGE, NEW YORK*, and said so in beaded letters sewn onto the tongues, were still paired neatly by the baseboard where the governess had left them when she eloped. She'd never come back for them, and as they were all that was left of her, Laura just let them sit there, advertising the pleasures of upstate. Why would Laura bother with abandoned moccasins in a dream about a swan-boy? So: not a dream?

He stirred, and groaned. His wing fanned a little against the floorboards. He was still in a state of shock or something. Maybe feverish. Maybe he was cold, even with the comforter. Suddenly Laura was aware of the smell, how very strong. Even if no one ever came upstairs this far, and if Nonna and Nonno were too old to smell much, someone might notice. It was hard to tell what the smell was like. Greasy, and nautical; sweet and clinically sour. A bit old people's nursing home. He just wasn't clean, that was the sorry truth of it.

A bath would warm him up. A bath would clean him up. Some of the smell would rinse down the drain. A bath wouldn't hurt the wing because swans swam in ponds and rivers and she was pretty sure that wings were treated with a kind of natural water repellent, like lanolin in sheep's wool. Like her good coat from Macy's.

She tiptoed into her bathroom and turned on the taps. The plastic plug leaked, but if you kept running the water every few moments you could keep the level topped up. She fit the plug into the drain.

It wasn't so improbable that Laura would be running a bath at this hour of a Tuesday morning. She didn't have to get ready to go to school, after all. Her grandparents were probably still asleep, or Nonno was up doing his toe-touching exercises in his one-piece buttoned underwear, and Nonna was saying her morning rosary in bed, propped up by about ninety pillows. Anyway they were deaf enough not to notice the running water, or so Laura told herself. They never talked to her until they all met downstairs in the dining room for breakfast or until Laura hollered "Ciao!" as she rushed by them and dashed off to school, most often on the late side. But never again, that.

When the tub was about two-thirds full, hot water vaporing the air and steaming the pink tiles, Laura turned off the taps. She returned to Miss Gianna Tebaldi's room. This was the hard part—how to wake him up enough to draw him into the bathroom and show him the hot water. She didn't want to frighten him and certainly didn't want him to make any noise.

It was impossible for her to imagine what would happen next if, say, he made some sort of fuss that alerted the household. She would have to go in the bathroom, close the door, and drown herself, and let everyone else sort it out.

"Lord above, is that a fish in the ceiling this morning?" called Mary Bernice. She was brisking about, making her usual racket to alert Nonno and Nonna that she had arrived and had the Medaglia D'Oro stewing in the fancy-pants Italian coffeepot.

That would be a great way to startle the visitor, a voice shrieking from a few floors away, but the swan-boy didn't stir. Laura was loath to inch forward and shake him by the shoulder in case he woke in a panic and attacked her. But she didn't have to try. Noiselessly Garibaldi must have streaked up the stairs once Mary Bernice released him from his imprisonment in the kitchen. He appeared so suddenly at Laura's ankle that she almost jumped. Taking one look at the interloper, the cat let out a dry sibilant warning, as if at another cat.

The swan-boy shook awake with a complex motion that Laura couldn't comprehend and couldn't describe. Some kind of shudder that rippled one way and then back the way it started, like a shook-out rug. His eyes clocked open in a single instant of alertness. His neck arched up and his head and face plunged forward. He hissed back at the cat out of the sides of his mouth somehow. Garibaldi just about had a coronary and fell down the stairs.

"Hi," said Laura. "Sorry—"

She wasn't sure what she was sorry for. She had rescued him, after all.

He took her in with a feral, almost a savage look. The face and neck and everything else were so human, but the look was avian; he turned his head and scrutinized her with his face in profile, first from one eye and then another, as if he had forgotten how to use them both together.

"I'm Laura."

He didn't say his name, maybe he couldn't speak, though that would be a problem. Or only speak swan. Swans didn't speak, did they, until they died, and then they sang a song. What song. Probably Bobby Vee's "Take Good Care of My Baby," if they had little swanlettes. Ducklings. Cygnets. Whatever they were called.

She was giggling, a nervous habit. He hissed again, but his head returned to a normal human position, and the sound was more experimental, tentative. A fourth-grade boy with a lisp trying out his first wolf whistle on the school playground.

"I'm okay, I'm no trouble, not to you anyway," she

said. She gestured to him: Come. She didn't want to touch him, nor did she think that would be correct. But her hand cupping toward herself as she backed away, he would understand that. A universal gesture, she hoped.

He did seem to understand. He let the coverlet slide off his shoulders. In the daylight he looked more—what was the word—common. Like someone who worked the shooting arcade at Coney Island, or trundled crates of pickled pepperoncini and balsamic vinegars down the sidewalks to the lift embedded in the sidewalk in front of Ciardi's Fine Foods and Delicacies. Like a *contadino,* only not dark-roasted like southern Italian farmers. Bleached, fair, nearly blond. The swan-eyes were Nordic ice-green. Not at all warm. He put his right hand upon the windowsill and pulled himself to his bare feet. His wing, now she could see it in daylight, went down to just above his ankle.

Come, she gestured. "*Vieni con me.*" Though why should he know Italian, he looked more like a Dutchman or a Swede. "Come," she said, and extended her hand, as if it were a kind of wing. She backed away onto the top step so he could pass before her down the short hall to the bathroom door on the left.

He shrugged and grunted, no particular language but that of effort and ache. He did as she proposed.

He walked by and swept by. His human shoulder near her, the wing on his left side away. It brushed the wall and made a sound like Mrs. Steenhauser sweeping her back steps with that old broom she used. He seemed to know what Laura meant, because he didn't go as far as her room or the box room in the front of the house, but paused and looked in the bathroom door. The expression on his face was unreadable.

She came up behind him, murmuring, but his wing made him seem wider than, say, John Greenglass or Sam Rescue. The hall was narrow and she couldn't get around him. Finally she said, "Well, go on in?" with a lilt in her voice, as if she were Nonna saying, Won't you try one of my biscotti?

"Ah," he said, in a normal voice. Luckily, downstairs a clock was chiming—it was 7:30, not 7:00 A.M. as she had guessed. He went in and turned to look over his shoulder—well, you'd have to say his wing. Laura put her finger to her lips. She didn't know if this was a universal symbol for *shhhhh* or just high school study hall, but he gave a bit of a nod, and moved into the room.

Then the noise of steps coming up the stairwell from the hall below. It wasn't Mary Bernice, she walked more lopsidedly with that hip, off the beat; nor could it be Nonno or Nonna, because neither of them could move so quickly. "Hey up there, morning glory," called someone, must be John Greenglass. "We know you're up because we heard the pipes—are you decent? We're coming up to take a quick glance at the work we did yesterday. All clear?"

She panicked, but could hardly say *no*—she was supposed to be in the bathroom. "Make it snappy," she called, and shut the bathroom door behind her and locked it, and made the *shhhh* sign to the swan-boy again, more urgently than before. This time the swan-boy nodded in response, no doubt about it.

The noise of feet on the stairs. John and Sam both, it seemed. The swan-boy, now half turned toward Laura, undid his tunic with one hand. The buttons were broad flat irregular discs. At first Laura thought they might be dials cut from the bough of a tree, but she then realized they were probably sliced with a hacksaw from the antler of a deer, and someone had drilled holes in them to take the thread.

The five front buttons slipped out of their loose buttonholes easily enough. Then the swan-boy's hand went to his opposite shoulder, and Laura saw that the tunic was attached across his left shoulder by two more buttons joining a top seam. So that was how he could be dressed while sporting a wing that could fit in no human sleeve.

Once unbuttoned at the clavicle, the blue tunic fell

to the floor in one piece, like an orange peel if you do it just so. He wore no undershirt. The swan-boy made a quarter-turn out of modesty, perhaps, and with the flick of his wrist pulled out the slipknot of his belted trousers. They dropped to his ankles. He was naked without them, pink and raw and about as perfectly formed a young man as the Renaissance liked to paint them, if you could discount the monstrous wing.

Laura knew nothing of the male form except from museums. It had been too long since she had seen Marco, and of course she'd never seen him in such a revelation. The *Twelve Questions and Answers for Young People About Becoming Adults* brochure, so favored by all the biology teachers at Driscoll, was replete with diagrams of human-shaped mannikins. But the artists had mostly fudged the details, skipping right from silhouetted growth charts of standard-issue humans, from birth to twenty-five, to close-up diagrams of male piping and female pockets. Too little attention (meaning none) was paid to the surface details and the interest that was presumed to exist between them.

Even of the female body Laura could draw little inference. Girls in locker rooms were either bold and brassy or they dressed under towels and slips. The easygoing type made fun of the prudes, who consequently didn't even look at themselves, much less anyone else.

It was hard to draw conclusions about normal looks when you never looked. All you could examine was yourself in the glass, and who didn't look fairly fake and even suspicious in her own bathroom mirror? The embarrassed, unconfident breasts, the untutored softness everywhere.

A rap on the door. John. "Hey, Laura—sorry to pester you, but what is the deal with that smell? Just asking in case it's a sign of more trouble up here. I was pretty sure we got it all yesterday, but boy, is that a stink and a half."

"I'm—I'm dyeing some clothes, it must be the dye," said Laura, proud of being able to think up a lie, and able to deliver it without stuttering.

"Well, smells like something died in there all right. Okay, we're checking the roof. We'll be done in a jif."

The swan-boy had frozen at the sound of their voices on the other side of the door. Laura was only two feet from him. This was probably illegal and Father Chiumiento would certainly raise both his hands in front of his cheeks at the thought of it. How could she even express such a moment the next time she was in the confessional, kneeling on that leathery pad behind the dark brown velvet drape? I helped a naked young man into the bathtub. That was probably more than ten thousand venials, maybe even a big fat black blotch of a mortal sin on her soul. But to get forgiveness for such a transgression she had to be able to confess it, and she couldn't imagine how.

"Come," she said softly, and touched him lightly on his elbow.

He inched forward. His wing elevated slightly to help him retain his balance as he gripped the side of the old clawfoot. Once he'd stepped in, and managed his second foot, he swiveled his round rump to the taps and his face to the door, so his wing could fall out of the tub and not get so wet. Maybe the water was the right temperature for the boy part but too hot for the swan part. In any case, the falling forward of the wing provided a sort of shower curtain allowing, indeed enforcing, a modicum of respectability. He sat down. She didn't stop watching.

The grit swirled off him in rings like mud off a submerged boot. He closed his eyes with the blessing of warm water, and murmured "*Tak . . . Danke schön,*" and then, a moment later, in a rough but intelligible accent, "Thank you."

"Thank *you,*" she replied, the nonsense weirdness of Catholic politeness getting the better of her. But it was what she meant, very truly.

14

Then came the awkwardness. She daren't stare at him, but there was hardly anyplace else to look. She couldn't leave—John and Sam were still monkeying about in the box room just a few feet down the hall. She sat on the toilet and put her head in her hands, and she let her glance slant down and sideways. The floor was tiled in black and white hexagons that could give you an optical illusion headache if you stared at them.

He was breathing out in long puffs. Frankly even his breath smelled bad, like a fishmonger's blooded apron. She thought about adding a dollop of Mr. Bubble to the bath, but it was too late to propose it, and maybe too girlish. Then, thinking about soap, she stood up and turned to the sink. Intending not to look at him in the mirror, she looked anyway; she saw his articulated spine and the strong shoulders of a boy who maybe could partly fly, and the luscious skin, flushed rosy by the hot water, and spattered with an up-tilting, linear constellation of small darker freckles. In so looking she caught an unexpected glimpse of herself in the mirror, for almost the first time, and all she could tell of herself was that she looked hungry. She picked up the bar of white soap and turned and cleared her throat. He swiveled his head and she held it out to him. He took it as if it were a sandwich, or a secret, and held it in front of his face and looked at it, and smelled it. What did Ivory really smell like, she wondered. Like the inside of a washing machine. But that was comparing like to like, Miss Parsley commented in Laura's head: Comparing Ivory bar soap to the residue of Ivory flakes doesn't get us anywhere.

The swan-boy seemed to get the point of soap, and dropped the chalky-rubbery bar into the water. Then Laura handed him a yellow rubber duck from the five-and-dime. He squeezed it and it quacked, which made him laugh—a male laugh, unmistakable. She flushed the toilet quickly to try to disguise the noise. John and Sam sounded as if they were hanging out the window, inspecting their work, and luckily they didn't hear the swan-boy. She put her finger to her lips again and scowled and he raised his eyebrows and grimaced. A universal gesture for *oops,* maybe. *Sorry.*

Still sitting, still sheathed by his forward-raking wing, he began to wash with the soap and then the intimacy really was intolerable. Sam and John were done in the box room and tramping back and forth across the hallway to the top of the stairs, presumably removing their supplies. "All clear," called John Greenglass as they started to evacuate the attic floor.

"When you come down, I'll tell you about Fluster this morning," called Sam Rescue.

Phew. Relief. When they were well and truly on the floor below, and not returning, Laura turned and looked at the swan-boy. She said, "*Parli italiano?* Or English?"

"*Dansk, tysk,*" he replied. "And yes, *engelsk.* English. Some little-time *engelsk.*" The accent was anything but Italian. More like soft vocal clapping.

"Okay, down to brass tacks then. What is your name?"

He looked puzzled. "What is your name?" She thought he was repeating the question to understand it, but when he rolled his hand, the one with the toy duck in it, she realized he was asking her.

"I am Laura," she said, pointing to herself, as if there were several other girls in the bathroom. "You?"

"I am Hans," he said.

Laura, Hans. Hans, Laura. That was that then. It seemed to Laura that there was nothing else to say, except this: "Does it hurt?" Pointing to the drapery of the wing.

"Everywhere," he said. "*Overalt.*" He ran his dripping fingers from the top rack of bridal-white feathers, at the place where they pinned into his human skin, to the round of his shoulder, and then behind his head to the nape of his neck.

It was too much to look at, to think about. Pain *overalt.* "I have to do something about these clothes," she said. "They stink to high heaven. The cook will be up here with the plumbers if not the police. I have to wash them or get rid of them, something."

Even as Laura spoke, Nonna was hollering up the stairwell. "*Laura?* What is that unholy smell? Are you unwell? Do you want me to ask Dr. Buechlein to pay a call?"

Again with the lies, they were just fountaining up out of Laura this morning. She opened the door and replied, calmly as possible, "Sorry, Nonna. The cat came up and got sick. I'm cleaning it up."

"What did that cat eat, a rotten rat?" asked Nonna, but she sounded mollified. "I'll send up Mary Bernice with a bucket of water and ammonia."

"Don't," said Laura, fiercely. "I said I'll take care of it."

Nonna began her way down the steps toward her breakfast. "First we have Noah's flood in the ceiling, and now a beached whale in the attic. Does Jesus want us to suffer so? I can't think that this is fair, with my sister and her great catch Mr. Corm Kennedy coming tomorrow evening. If we have to take them round the corner to Panetta's because the house is uninhabitable, all is lost. We'll be celebrating Christmas with the Bowery bums or *gli indigenti* at the soup kitchen. Now I have to make the *scialatelli* this morning and, Laura, I don't want my noodles to pick up the stench of vomited rat."

"I'll *handle* it, Nonna!"

"The excitement of the Nativity is getting to her, Ovid, you can hear it in her voice." Nonna's words were broadcast downstairs to her husband, who must already be at the breakfast table. "She's being rude. The young always get so overexcited at this time of year."

"These can't stay here, or you'll be found out," said Laura to Hans. She picked up his clothes. "I will wash them later if I can sneak them downstairs. For now—do you mind?" Hans looked as if he didn't understand, but he shrugged. A shrug to which a trailing wing is attached expressed a more mighty class of bewilderment than Laura had ever conceived. It was just so intense.

She picked up the tunic and the trousers and folded them into as small a bundle as she could. She wrapped them in her striped bath towel.

"I'll be right back," she said. "Stay. Stay here. Stay quiet. You know how to stay?"

He didn't answer at first. "I do not know how to leave," he replied at last.

"I'll be right back."

He squeaked the duck at her.

She closed the door behind her so carefully that the tongue of the doorknob mechanism hardly clicked in its slot. All the other human life in the house had settled to the bottom floors. She ran on tiptoes into Miss Gianna Tebaldi's old room. Garibaldi was there, making inroads into the discarded lasagne. Laura took Miss Gianna Tebaldi's old metal clothes hamper, once painted a pretty lime green and now spotted with a pox of rust. She crammed the offending clothes and the towel inside and she shut the lid. Then she opened the window and set the whole hamper out onto the fire escape. Several pigeons hobbled on the rail to investigate, got a whiff, thought better of it, and flew away.

When she went back into the bathroom, he was just beginning to stand. Having shucked off his pelt of dirt, he was beginning to regain some sense of propriety, and he turned his regal back to her, hiding his nakedness like Adam.

"Sit right back down there," she said, "we have to do your hair. It's an absolute fright."

He obeyed, but complained, "The water, cold and full of dirt and salt."

"I'll let some water out and we'll refill. Here's a tin pail from the Jersey shore. I fill it up and rinse my hair with it." She knelt at the tub toward the end with the plug, and tugged at the chain. The water began to gurgle out, leaving lines of sediment on the porcelain as the level dropped. She kept her eyes glued to the drain. Custody of the senses, Laura. With her peripheral vision, however, she could tell that he had arranged his one hand like a human fig leaf in the place where fig leaves usually find themselves. A gentleman, she thought. A gentle-swan.

Using her blue bucket with the white seashells painted around the rim, she washed his hair for him. She lavished upon him dollops of shampoo. She rinsed and rinsed, all the while refilling the tub and letting it out. The shampoo sudsed up the bathwater, which was growing cleaner with the repeated drainings and refills. Finally the slick of shampoo was mostly gone, and even in a room without a window, his hair appeared bright as rings of shaved sunlight. He looked at her and smiled. “Never before,” he said.

“Me either.”

15

There was the problem of nakedness. Laura was already figuring out that she could probably commandeer the washing machine when Mary Bernice went out to do the morning shopping. "Popping round to the shops," she always said, when she meant haunting the little Greek grocery where the complacent owner sat on a stool by the door and watched out for riffraff pinching the wares, and the tall thin wife with the wobbly arms ran back and forth grabbing things for people as if they couldn't read labels for themselves. It could take Mary Bernice an hour to get the most basic stuff, tuna fish and Bab-O and olives and revolting hard-boiled eggs in glass jars, because she liked the exhausted Greek wife and felt bad for her and talked to her about missing the old country. Apparently they could make common cause in nostalgia, even if their old countries were on the kitty-corner opposite ends of the puzzle-piece map of Europe.

Once the cook had left, Laura would squirrel down the stairs and wash Hans's storm-drenched clothes. She could get them done with the washer and into the dryer before Mary Bernice returned. Those rags wouldn't smell so bad after spending a hot rinse cycle improved by a cup of Tide powder. But in the meantime, the bath was over and Hans had to get out, and though the furnace was working overtime it was still late December during a cold snap. He had to wear *something.* Laura's towel was outside on the fire escape. The only thing she had big enough to clothe nakedness was her own nightgown, which she still had on, and a scratchy old bathrobe with large white polka dots on a pink background. For so many reasons, neither of those outfits would suit him.

"Wait here again," she said. "Wait."

"Cold," he said. He was starting to shiver. That was probably a sign of improving circulation. She thought of the coverlet and grabbed that. He could use it as a towel and maybe she could run it through the dryer later. "I'll be right back," she said. "Can you be quiet?"

"I can be nothing," he said, which caught her heart in her throat, until he finished, "but quiet."

She leaped down the stairs two at a time. One level below, her grandmother's sewing room stood in the back of the house. It faced the fire escape and the backyard and Mrs. Steenhauser's backyard. Next to the sewing room was the master bathroom, and forward of that, her grandparents' bedroom, which looked out into Van Pruyn Place. You could get into their bathroom from the hall or the bedroom. She opened the hall bathroom door very slowly, just in case she had misunderstood everyone's whereabouts and Nonno was still shaving. But he wasn't. The moist air smelled of old man, stinky-sweet, and also of bay lime splash. On the back of the door Laura hoped to find Nonno's bathrobe, a great, belted prehistoric cloak of some weirdly fluffy, camel-colored yardage. Nonno often wore it down to breakfast, but he must be in a hurry to get to the shop this morning. The last day or two before Christmas were among the busiest days of the year for Ciardi's Fine Foods and Delicacies. So here was the precious robe, ready for filching. It was still a little warm from big old Nonno. Well, good.

Back upstairs, she said gingerly, "Can you put this on by yourself?"

Hans had stepped out of the tub and was mostly decent in the coverlet. He looked at Nonno's bathrobe. "*En frakke?*" he ventured, and corrected himself. "Sorry. I try to English. A coat?"

"Close enough. You could put your arm in this side and sort of just, you know, drape the other sleeve maybe down in front? It's so big. The belt would go under your wing and keep the robe closed around your waist. For warmth and—privacy. For now. I'll find you something else soon. Yes?"

"Where is this place?" he said, almost to himself, but it was English so of course it was to her, too. "Yes," he answered.

Laura might be going to Montreal but she didn't want to go to hell, too, so she helped Hans keep the coverlet cinched at his waist. She wasn't ready to be this close to a naked creature any larger than Garibaldi. When she imagined Nonna showing up at the bathroom door, she almost felt faint, but there was no reason to scare herself silly, because that nightmare could never happen. Nonna's bad knees, the acute angle of the attic staircase.

Hans shimmied his arm into the right sleeve and used his teeth to draw the collar closer to his shoulder. Laura pulled the back of the robe around as Hans lifted his wing. He found one end of the sash and she brought up the other, and when she had made sure the front panels of the robe were overlapping and cozy and dignified, she tied the sash in place. It was like helping some of her first graders get their snowsuits on.

Then at least he was dressed, he was decent, he was clean. The bathtub was a wreckage of silt, however. It looked like the tub at the shore house after she'd been playing at the beach all day. She'd have to take care of that later. Now, she gripped him by the hand and led him to her bed. "I need to go eat breakfast or they'll wonder," she said. "I'll be back as soon as I can. I'll bring you some fruit and bread and cheese and maybe a bowl of Maypo."

He didn't hear her. He had put his head on her pillow. His tender clean pink feet arched. His tide-green eyes went vague, and she felt herself going invisible in his sight. Not an unfamiliar feeling for Laura. Before she'd backed up to reach for her own slippers, his eyes had closed. Still on the bathroom floor, the coverlet was wet on one side but the other side was dry. She retrieved it, turned it over and fluffed it upon him, and she hurried downstairs before anyone got suspicious. The bad smell was lifting.

In the front hall, John Greenglass and Sam Rescue were putting down drop cloths and setting up ladders with a board across them so they could reach the ceiling. Nonno was armoring himself in his thick wool coat. His grey scarf, his grey hat with a green parrot feather in the band, his leather gloves. "You're early, Nonno," said Laura.

"You late," he said, teasingly. "Shipment of figs in honey come in this morning, before shop open, and our poor Matteo don't multiply by dozens so he can't count for check bill of lading. You come by today, help out on floor?"

"I'm not sure. I don't feel ready."

"Why not, you fifteen. You addled enough."

"I might need to help Nonna roll out the pasta."

"She let you help, I ring up *Corriere della Serra* and Vatican and tell them, Christmas miracle." He kissed her and touched her face with his gloved hand, which felt tender and distant at the same time. The world outside the open front door, when he left, was bright and white but clear. Shine adhered to the surfaces; ice polished the brownstones.

"So our owl," began Sam Rescue. "Didn't let her go yesterday, because of the weather report. Such high winds last night, poor thing would've been blown to Buffalo. But she's eating better. I tried to feed her some herring but she turned her head. But she liked some smoosh of persimmon my auntie gave her on a spoon. She flapping her wings stronger. Wants to go, doesn't like that wooden milk crate I got her caged in. But we gotta wait till a better day."

Laura, in a hurry to get her breakfast, and some for Hans, and rush back upstairs, paused anyway to say, "What makes a better day?"

"You know it when you see it, child," said Sam.

"Stir the primer, Sam, and rest your tongue, or we'll be here all morning," said John Greenglass.

"I have to have my breakfast or they'll kill me," said Laura.

"They would never do that. They might wound you, but they wouldn't finish you off," muttered John. "They're not so bad."

She didn't stick around to press the point. The dining room was cleared already so she bounced downstairs to the kitchen. Mary Bernice was there, looking aggrieved, while Nonna bashed about the kitchen, assembling bowls and ingredients. "There you are, Laura; what a morning to dawdle! Late for breakfast. You cleaned up that awful mess upstairs that I was smelling, I hope. I thought it was sewage backing up. Just the way to welcome our guests tomorrow night. Put them off their dinner. Mary Bernice, the eggs, the eggs, the eggs, you have only four eggs? *Sei pazza?*"

"I'll pick up some more this morning when I make my rounds."

"Miss Agnes places a telephone call to me this morning, Laura; so many ladies needing their perms, she is opening two hours early today. She reschedules me to come in at eight-fifteen. So we'll do the pasta later. Your grandfather is bringing the fish home tomorrow morning but the eels come tonight. So today is the pasta and the antipasti platters, and we'll have time to set the table. Mary Bernice will hang the mistletoe, or we'll ask one of those boys upstairs. We'll have to do the fish and the profiteroles tomorrow. It'll be a peasant's day of work but we'll strike it rich. *Gesù* wouldn't dare give up on us now, not when we've come so far."

"Jesus isn't known for taking direction, not in my church," murmured Mary Bernice.

Nonna had no time to argue. She was running through the shopping needs and consulting her recipes, scrawled in Italian. For this meal, Mary Bernice was sidelined, which made the cook cross. "*Festa dei sette pesci,* Mary Bernice."

"I know, the feast of the seven fishes, you tell me seven times already."

"I already picked up the dried salt cod; don't tell Signore Ciardi but it's the Portuguese brand. We'll soak it when I get back. Also we can do the shrimp tonight and keep them in the icebox. The calamari, the mussels, they come tomorrow; and the fresh eels! They come into de Gonzague's today in those tray-boxes.

We'll do the smelts at the last minute in olive oil, my my. And finally, this year, lobster tails."

"Lobster tails!" said Mary Bernice. "Plated in gold leaf, by the sound of it?"

"Yes," said Nonna, "and we're going to ornament them with Mr. Corm Kennedy's initials in little diamonds. Mind your business, Mary Bernice. I don't see the yellow onions or the cremini."

"Pantry," said Mary Bernice. Opening the Frigidaire, she waggled a forefinger. "You got your sour cream, your parmijohnny, your milk. This morning I'm collecting the courgettes and the purple thingy, the eggplant, *and* the carrots, *and* the store-bought bread crumbs. Leaving any minute now."

"Garlic, tinned anchovies, capers, green peppercorns in brine?"

"Pantry pantry pantry pantry."

Nonna looked put out. "I'm sure we're forgetting something, but I've read through my recipes twice. Well, we can always call Ovid to pick it up on his way home, that is, if there are any groceries still open. He'll keep late hours tonight."

"Go permanent your hair, Mrs. C., while they're holding you a chair."

"Laura, you'll help Mary Bernice if she gets back before I do?"

Laura nodded but added, "I have some things to do."

"Christmas surprises," said Mary Bernice. "Don't bother with my own personal Oldsmobile, Miss Laura, I'd have no place to park it on my block."

Nonna left the kitchen, huffing. Mary Bernice sat down and pulled out a pack of cigarettes. She put it quickly under her left haunch when Nonna swung through the door again. "But do we have enough salt for killing the eels, Mary Bernice? We don't want to run out."

"I got in four honking great canisters of salt, don't you be worrying about salt. See to your hair, now, and leave the prep work to me."

Nonna pulled on a plastic head scarf to protect her steel-grey chignon, wiped her eyeglasses on a paper towel, and left without further comment, though the silence was comment enough. Christmas cooking was a grim business.

Laura wanted nothing more than to cadge some breakfast for Hans, but she had to get Mary Bernice out the door, too. "When are you going shopping?" she asked.

"After you eat your hot cereal. I put it back on the stove since you were lollygagging this morning."

"I can get it for myself."

"Give me a chance to collect my wits." Mary Bernice

ladled out the Maypo and sat down across from Laura. "I have to set out my own campaigns for the day. How to do everything your bossy grandmother wants me to do, and how to keep my sanity while doing it. The stakes are higher this year, no getting around it."

"I know her sister is coming with the new husband, but we have company every Christmas Eve. Why is this so, so . . . extra?"

"It's the Mr. Corm Kennedy element."

"Is it that he's not Italian?"

"Not really. He's Irish, so he's Catholic, so that's not it either. It's that he's rich, see, and without meaning to gossip behind closed doors"—she leaned forward and lowered her voice, gossiping behind closed doors—"your grandfather is asking him to come in as a business partner. Put up some financing. Mr. Ovid's business is off, don't you know, and this house was probably a mistake, even if they got it at a bank auction. That's my understanding from little clues here and there. I keep my ears clean so I hear what I hear. Isabella thinks that if her sister and her fella come here and get a notion that the business is struggling, they won't invest. Your folks aren't lying by pulling out all the stops, mind; they just have a cash flow problem. In Las Vegas it's called going for broke, and in the bank they call it a bridge loan, but this isn't a bank, this is family. Why else do you think those poor lads are upstairs, painting and scraping away and dragging the little owls from the ceiling? To make the Ciardis look prosperous and able to carry all this off. To make the business look as if it's going full steam and no complaint. To make the investment look like a sound idea. They need Mr. Corm Kennedy's pretty pile of greenbacks to keep the outfit up and running."

"They've asked him already?"

"I believe Isabella asked her sister Geneva to ask him, and he hasn't given them an answer. But if he was offended or was going to say no, would they have accepted an invitation to dinner? I ask you. He lives up in Boston, you know, where they grow Kennedys by the dozen, all around Harvard Yard. Geneva hasn't been for a visit in too many years to count. She's showing her new man off to her big sister, and her big sister is trying to show off her nice house and the great business her husband started after the war. Christmas Eve, and all attention should be on the little Babe, but what are you going to do? They have to eat, and so do you. Are you done?"

"They're not doing this for *me*."

"And you think that convent school in Montreal is, what, a fleabag motel?"

"They asked Geneva and Mr. Corm Kennedy for

Christmas Eve long before I got thrown out of Driscoll."

"Yes, but your going away to board doesn't make things any easier. I'll say no more." She ground out her cigarette. "Do the washing up after yourself, Miss Laura, and I'll pop round to the shops in two shakes and a skiddle-skaddle."

Mary Bernice scooped up her coat and scarf and a tam-o'-shanter beanie that made her look like a plaid mushroom. After collecting the grocery carrier from the back storeroom, she dragged it through the kitchen toward the downstairs entrance under the front stoop. "I never asked you what that heavenly aroma was upstairs," she remarked, "and I don't think I want to know, but I hope you took care of it."

"I think it was the painting materials they're using."

"That's a crock of hooey, but I have no time to sort you out now. I'll be back soon as shank's mare can carry me."

After she had gone, Laura grabbed two apples, an orange, another bowl of Maypo and a spoon, and three Nabisco wafers. She raced upstairs. In the front hall, the workers had already installed a new puzzle-piece of ceiling, constructed out of prefabricated Sheetrock of some sort, and were busy applying grout to the seams. "For a girl on Christmas break she's in a mighty hurry," said John Greenglass. "She might have brought us a cup of New York coffee, don't you think, Sam?"

"Later," she called over her shoulder. Upstairs, she set down the breakfast and picked up the rejected lasagne, which Garibaldi had ravaged. She hoped he got sick on it. Then she retrieved the bad-smelling clothes from the fire escape and rushed down the back staircase with them. She plowed through the kitchen to the laundry room. She used one and a half cups of granulated Tide, hoping it would work. She added a healthy dribble of some other cleaning agent on the laundry shelf whose precise charms she couldn't understand from the label. It had a powerful antiseptic pong and was sure to do some good. The washer began to fill, the bubbles hid the clothes, chemistry went to work on the outfit that her dream had worn upon his arrival in her real life.

16

As she reached the first floor and catapulted toward the second, the doorbell rang.

"Well, *we're* not going to get it," called John Greenglass in a growly manner. He was lying on the plank applying that gunk to the ceiling with a trowel, and Sam Rescue was halfway up one of the ladders, holding backup supplies.

"Could be the owl's mother come looking for him," said Sam. Another wink.

She set the foods upon the hall table. *Mother:* the fault-line word, the three-alarm-fire word. A special mail delivery, a present from her mother. Then the thought: *mother*—raised in her a grassfire flame of hatred, anxiety, and need, tinder catching along her spine and racing to her roasting fingertips. She threw open the door as if going to battle.

The world glared so hard with sudden sun on snow that at first she only saw a silhouette in the spangle. Whoever it was, it wasn't Renata di Lorenzo Ciardi, arrived from the wilds of Albany County. "The hell do *you* want?" asked Laura.

"That's an unusual Christmas greeting," said Maxine Sugargarten. "Do you think Joseph said that to We Three Kings when they knocked on the stable door?"

"I mean it, I'm busy," said Laura.

"Can I come in," said Maxine, and came in without waiting for a reply. "Hi," she said to the guys on the ladders.

For privacy Laura would have taken Maxine into the dining room, but the pocket door was stuck in the wall because the floor had warped. The front room, with its big bay window and its wooden shutters folded neatly into the window woodwork, had functional doors. It wasn't set up as a parlor, which was one floor above it; it was mostly a kind of waiting room. Sometimes Nonno used it for store overstock if the tiny basement of Ciardi's Fine Foods was out of room. Today the front room held a Christmas tree and two or three fancy chairs Nonna had just picked up as a bargain in some church bazaar. The wallpaper showing the Bay of Naples was so new you could nearly smell the harbor. "Why did you come here?" asked Laura.

"I know why you're mad at me."

"You never came here before. We're not friends. What are you up to?"

Maxine unwrapped her long white scarf, as if expecting to be asked to sit down, and she tossed her chin high. She was practiced at that. The bandaged nose was grotesque. "Last night I heard that you got expelled because of attacking me. I thought you were only suspended."

Laura shrugged. It wasn't her job to clear up Maxine's confusion. "Where'd you pick up that good news?" she said, as if it weren't true.

"My big sister is going steady with Mr. G.'s son Raymond. Raymond told her, and she told me. I came to say I'm sorry about the whole thing."

"Nothing to do about it now," said Laura, "except I never meant to hit you in the face, by the way. That was an accident. So much blood, you probably can't believe me. I probably wouldn't believe you."

Maxine sighed with the self-effacing glory of the martyr. "I'm sorry about treating you like a moron. We were mean to you. We weren't nice."

"Is this news to you, because it isn't to me."

"We made you be late that day," said Maxine. She had something in her hands. It was a wrapped present. Oh please. "We started it. I know that. I feel terrible."

"You didn't make me steal your record."

"No, but we made you late for the class. We wanted to hear you stumble in your writing, just so we could laugh some more."

"I was late. *Fatto, capito.* Can you leave now, I have to be somewhere."

"No," said Maxine. "Mr. G. is always talking about honor, and I am trying to be honorable, even if you did slash my face with Bobby Vee. We made you late. Don't you get it? Donna Flotarde pulled over Doll Pettigrew's shower bench into the stall next to yours, and she climbed on it and while you were taking your shower she was leaning over the top of the partition."

"I know," said Laura. "I heard the bench scrape on the floor."

Maxine said the next part slowly, as if Laura were just off the boat. "She had a *bottle* of *shampoo* and she was leaking a very slow stream of it onto your *head* so it wouldn't rinse out in time. The rest of us were dressing or already dressed. We were making you have to stay in the shower so you would be the last one to arrive in English."

The thought of Donna Flotarde looking over the

top of the shower wall at Laura without any clothes on. "She's a bitch."

"She did it." Maxine Sugargarten heaved a great sigh. "But it was my idea. I set you up. Then when you got back at me, everything went out of control. I didn't mean for you to get expelled. So I'm sorry, so I'm here. I brought you a sorry present." Maxine looked as if she thought she deserved the Congressional Medal of Honor for the courage to confess her stupid crime.

"I don't want a present."

"I don't care, I want to give it to you. You can give it to somebody else."

"I hate Bobby Vee, just so you know."

"It isn't Bobby Vee. It's this new group called Peter Paul and Mary. They're really something else."

"You are a disgusting person," said Laura.

"I know that," said Maxine. "Don't rub it in. I don't have anything else to say."

"Then get out. And Merry Christmas."

She marched Maxine to the door but didn't slam it for fear of bringing down more of the ceiling. "Well, that was brisk," said John Greenglass.

"Here's a record album you can have. Peter Paul and Polly or something like that."

"No thanks," said John. "I prefer good ole Johnny Cash."

"I'm more a Nina Simone fellow," said Sam, "or Sam Cooke. Anyway, it's all wrapped up for you, it's a present from that white girl."

"*I'm* a white girl."

"You know what I mean," said Sam. "She extra white."

The record album had its uses; it could be a tray for carrying the food upstairs for Hans. "So long, fellows."

"You're in a really good mood today," called Sam. "Better hang that mistletoe quick so I can steal a kiss and cheer you up some."

17

She brought the breakfast into her bedroom. Light was slanting in across the FDR Drive and across Queens, light from way out over the cold green Atlantic. On the faded wallpaper on the far side of Laura's room it cast a mottled overlay because those windows it passed through sure could use a washing.

The light skipped over the bed. In sedate shadow Hans, in Nonno's robe, lay on his stomach. His wing was retracted, covering part of his back and the top of his legs, like a huge fan. His face was turned toward the door that Laura had entered. His arm lay on the bed beside him. His eyes were closed and gummy, as if he'd been crying in his sleep.

Laura set down the record album–breakfast tray. She pulled from the corner a small wicker chair afflicted with a lazy leg—you had to sit in it with care or it could give out. Here she perched, just out of the light, and kept a sort of morning vigil. The light inched along. Soon enough the shaft of morning fell upon his hand. The hand—his only hand—was lovely to look at. Clean now, it lay beside him, turned open to the ceiling, and its thumb curled into the palm. A strong hand—the pump of flesh at the base of the thumb was rounded like a bulb of fennel. The top of the hand had roughly the same articulation as his behind, which now that he was asleep Laura could dare to acknowledge she had *seen*. She had seen a naked young man, at least from the back. His caboose, his *culo*. She could tell under the drape of Nonno's robe what was there and what it looked like, and how it resembled the open, waiting hand. This realization was calming and shocking at once.

The hand was pink; she wanted to rest something in it. A seashell. A strawberry. An owl feather. Her lips—to sink her lips there and let him cup a kiss from her without knowing it.

She was becoming demented. She couldn't sit here and gawk all day. It was probably against the law, even in the privacy of her grandparents' home. In any case it was, as Nonna straight from deportment class might say, unseemly.

"Are you awake?" she asked. She could use a normal voice now; the repair guys were two flights down and banging away at something with hammers, and everyone else in the house was gone except Garibaldi, whom she had again closed in the kitchen. "Shouldn't you wake up and eat something?"

He stirred, the slightest of movements, a dawn wind in the sawgrass at the Jersey shore. His eyes opened. She waited for him to smile but he did not smile.

"Are you awake?" she said again, inching the chair forward. It buckled and sent her on her knees. He changed the angle of his wing and rolled on his side, and used his right arm to push himself to a sitting position. He rubbed his eyes with his fist. It must be hard to rub your left eye with your right fist.

"I brought you something to eat," she said, feeling servile, on her knees and all that. She sat back on her heels as if she'd *intended* to kneel, thank you very much, like a Japanese maiden in some kind of tea ceremony.

"This is nothing to eat," he said, looking at it and looking away. "*Affald*." She felt obscurely affronted by his tone but kept on.

"Where did you come from?" she asked.

"Where did *you* come from?" he replied.

"Were you flying?" she said. "How could you fly with one wing?"

"I don't remember," he said. "I was blown in the dark, and struck something. I thought it was a rock in the sea, but I wake up in these rooms. Did you collect me from some island in the ocean?"

"No," she said. "You were just here."

"And *you* were just here." He looked around and yawned. "Who is this?" He lifted his wing and used the tip of it like a finger, to point at a picture frame on the wall behind her. "Is this your *kæreste*? Your boyfriend, your beau?"

She didn't have to turn her head to know he wasn't pointing to the framed picture of the Sacred Heart of Jesus, the Lord Himself indicating His own spooky luminescent heart beneath His Jesus toga. Hans meant the other picture on the adjacent wall. "That, no, that's not my boyfriend," she said, lowering her eyes. "That's my—that's Marco."

"Marco."

"Marco."

He waited.

"Marco Ciardi. My brother."

"You have a brother." He chewed over this, glancing at the photograph several times, and back at Laura, as if to catch the resemblance.

"I *had* a brother," she said.

"I think I had brothers, too," he said. "And a sister."

"You think?"

"I am not certain where I am or what has happened. Or who you are, really."

She said, "Well, I'm Laura Maria Ciardi. This is where I live. Upper East Side Manhattan. Yorkville. For a little while longer anyway."

He ran his hand along the outer ridge of his feathers, smoothing them down.

"How come you flew into my roof?" she asked.

He made a face of incomprehension.

She tried again, working for a more storybook tone. "How did you come to crash into my house?"

"I cannot tell you." At first she thought he was saying he didn't have the language, but his expression clarified the matter: he didn't have the thoughts. The memories. Perhaps they'd been knocked out of him by the impact of his arrival outside her window. That must be a frightening thing.

"You were lucky not to be speared on one of the pointy tops of the Queensboro Bridge." He looked blank. She busied herself tucking her nightgown under her calves so her legs were merely a package of cottony roses. "Was your sister a younger sister?"

But he only shook his face and used his one hand to hide both his eyes, an ineffectual strategy. Then he thought better of it and raised his wing instead. It made a more effective screen.

"I'm sorry," she said. "Some breakfast would help."

She wanted to give him a telling. It would go something like:

She sat on her bed next to him and laid the wing of the trembling boy in her lap. I know about you, she said in a soft and doctorly voice. You are one of the Wild Swans, you are the youngest brother whose sister failed to finish the shirtsleeve that would turn you back into a full boy. You must have found some way to fly away. Maybe your sister made you an artificial wing out of a stout tree branch and a thick woolen blanket. And then he turned to her with his tear-filled eyes and fell upon her shoulder, and she held him.

But she couldn't say any of that. It sounded nutso. They'd commit her to an asylum someplace, some brooding brick prison with locked doors on the ward, and soft bad food served with plastic utensils.

"I wonder," she tried, "if you are famous?"

He didn't understand.

"You are in a story."

This seemed to make him angry. “Everyone is in a story.”

She tried to mimic that expression of his, the raising of eyebrows and the shrug, as if to say, So what? “So tell me your story,” she suggested.

“I don’t know how a story goes, I don’t know my own story. Tell me *your* story and I’ll see if I can learn how to do it.”

Ah, but she’d never told her story, not really. Mary Bernice knew some of it, and Nonno and Nonna knew all of it, but not what it meant to her. Not how it felt. Because stories, maybe, were drafts of reality based on feelings. Oh, what a Miss Parsley thing to say. Maybe Laura had been paying attention more than she knew.

She didn’t know where to start—with the first mollusk, the first Ciardi back in Salerno, how Nonno and Nonna emigrated a thousand years ago, arriving just in time for the Great Depression? She couldn’t really tell their stories. Even though she lived with them, her grandparents were to her as holy mysteries.

“You had parents,” he prompted her, “unless perhaps you didn’t?”

“I did,” she admitted. “My father was Giuseppe Victor Emmanuel Ciardi. Called Joe. He was born in Rome and raised in Little Italy, here in New York, in the house where his parents lived until about five years ago. He married my mother before the war. She was Renata di Lorenzo till she got married. She sounds like a movie star like that, but she became ordinary Mrs. Ciardi. They were just Joe and Rennie Ciardi. They had a baby boy a year or two before my father went off to boot camp. That's Marco, that's my brother." She pointed over her shoulder. She still didn't look at the photo, but she didn't have to. She knew it by heart—every corpuscle of red blood in her body had his face stamped upon it.

"Marco," he said.

"My father came home after the end of the war, hugged his growing boy, but he wanted a career in the military. He went to Europe. Austria. We were going to follow. My mother was pregnant with me. He died there, an infection, far away across the world. It was after the war, you see. The big war."

She had expected him to be sympathetic, or sad for her, but all he said was: "I like the sound of far away across the world."

"I hate that sound," she told him. "So I was born, picture this, after my father was already dead. We lived in a flat upstairs from my grandparents near Mulberry and Hester. My mother, my brother, and me. Then, five years ago, the same month that my grandparents were moving here, something happened to my brother."

"What happened to Marco?"

He got blown out to sea.

The things she could never say to anyone ordinary, like a Maxine or a Miss Parsley or even a Mary Bernice. Laura tried to say them anyway. "He and a friend were in a small plane that left LaGuardia in a fog. They were on their way to an air show in Pawtucket, Rhode Island. Their plane crashed in the Sound forty minutes later."

Hans repeated "crashed in the Sound" as if it were a phrase of wicked enchantment. Did he make any sense of airplanes, was he just humoring her? What did she really know of airplanes for that matter? He just shook his head. "Crashed in the Sound. But what happened to him?"

She wiped her nose on the back of her hand. "They never found him."

"So he might come back one day?"

"They found parts of the plane. Weeks later. In Connecticut."

"Oh." He looked at her with an evenness both dry and horrific. "I see."

"My mother couldn't stand the second loss. She went into a padlocked ward in some hospital and when she got out she couldn't come back and live with her in-laws and me. She went back upstate where she comes from. She lives there now with her mother. Nonna di Lorenzo. Some town on the Hudson River. East Greenbush. I don't see my mother. She doesn't come to visit. I live with Nonno and Nonna, at least for now. But I'm moving to Montreal."

He seemed not to know where Montreal was, but then, she hardly did either.

"That's my story," she said. "My grandparents love me but they are getting rid of me because I'm a bad influence on the other girls in school. I guess. Can you give me your story now?"

That was something he couldn't do. Faced with her life, Hans's life seemed even thinner. He was like something made of paper and air. He held out his wing to one side and his arm to the other. Nonno's bathrobe was way too big for him, and now Laura was able to pick up a kick of Old Spice and also a hint of stale sweat seeping from the ample folds. "Here I am," said Hans. "That's all the story I have. I am here."

18

Before that impossible story in her head—that she could console Hans somehow—could come to pass in reality, the sound of the workers rose up the stairwell. They arrived at the bottom of the attic flight and readied to clomp up to the top.

Laura put her finger to her lips and made a look of panic at Hans. She flew to her doorway. She swiveled the door till it was only open an inch, and called out, "What do you think you're doing now?" She sounded just like Nonna.

"Hey there, Miss Laura," said Sam. "We bringing up supplies to put in the box room."

"You can't do that, I'm not dressed! What supplies? Who told you you could? Leave me alone."

They paused. Laura had been more than eager to

loiter on the outskirts of their work zone earlier. "It's the strapping and a few of the panels of Sheetrock we're going to need to redo the master bedroom," called John, warily, as if he didn't see why she needed to know.

"What the hell are you *talking* about?" She didn't care what they were talking about but she had to keep them from taking another step. By now she was at the top of the staircase, flapping in her nightgown. In this ankle-length garment she'd already walked by them twice this morning, so her sudden attack of propriety wasn't believable, even to her.

They propped the Sheetrock on the bottom stairs and looked up at her much, she supposed, as they had looked at the baby white owl in the ceiling. Get a load a this, will ya?

With patience probably born of many sessions with excitable lady clients, John Greenglass said, "Let me tell you what we're up to. The leak we finally plugged in the coping beneath your windowsill? It drained down the front wall of the building. For some reason it erupted a little in your grandparents' bedroom and yellowed their ceiling and stained the wallpaper between their windows. That new wallpaper we just installed at Thanksgiving. Then the drip somehow bypassed the parlor on the floor below that. It traveled along some hidden track in the lathing on that floor and finished up down in the front hall, where as you know it ran across a beam and emerged as a heavy drip in the hall ceiling. We've found and plugged the original breach outside your window. We've finished repairing the downstairs ceiling for today, and we'll be back tomorrow morning to give it a couple of quick coats before that party tomorrow night. It'll smell of paint, but your grandmother says it's the feast of the little fishies or something, so the smell of dinner will hide it somewhat. As for your grandparents' bedroom, they don't want us to start repair today. After Christmas we'll come back and do what need's doing. Before she left Mrs. C. told us to store this strapping and wallboard and crud in the box room. Do we have clearance to pass? We'll be quick."

"Leave it there and I'll bring it up," said Laura.

Sam said, "Miss Laura, you can't shift these sons of . . . They heavy as the wages of sin. Just let us by and we be outa your hair in two minutes flat. If you're feeling shy, go in your room and we won't bother you there."

"You can't," she said. "I'm sorry I'm such an inconvenience to you."

But really, she thought, I'm mostly an inconvenience to myself.

They started up the stairs anyway, John in front. "In and out in a jif, you'll see."

She fled back to her room and slammed the door shut. She had thought Hans might be terrified, but he looked relaxed and curious. He was too dazed, she realized, to be frightened. She covered her mouth with her hand and pointed at him. He covered his mouth, too, but his eyes were laughing at her. Too much drama.

This couldn't go on. He couldn't live here. He hadn't eaten much yet, he was mostly naked, and the house would be crawling with people from now till the day after Christmas, at least. She had to find some other place for him to stay.

While she was waiting for John and Sam to finish bashing about in there, she slipped to her shallow closet. It was only a bump-out in the hall because there was no space in her room for it. She couldn't spend the day in her nightgown. She pulled out her shirtwaist dress with the large polka dots in turquoise and iodine yellow. They floated serenely on an ivory field. It was decent enough without being flashy. Back in her room, she grabbed from her dresser a pair of black tights and the necessaries, as Mary Bernice called them: some panties, a girdle, and a bra so sensible that even a nun could sport it without becoming an occasion of sin.

"Finishing up now, we'll leave you alone," called John when they were done.

"We'll be back tomorrow to give the downstairs ceiling its final coat," added Sam. "Don't be a stranger, stranger."

"Who are they?" whispered Hans as they descended deeper in the house.

"Greenglass and Rescue," she replied. She didn't want to call them John and Sam. That would sound way too familiar. "I have to get dressed."

When she got back from her bathroom, he was standing with his back to the room, looking out her window. She crossed the floor and stood next to him. She tried to see if Van Pruyn Place was pretty or pretty ugly. Looking through new eyes wasn't as easy as it sounded, though. Directly across the street, the brownstones took on a lurid pink tinge in the sunlight. She saw where a violinist of some orchestra or other was sitting in front of a music stand in his kitchen, vigorous in his wifebeater and gabardines, practicing to beat the band. (Ha! A violinist beating the band.) The taller buildings beyond, over on the avenue, looked as if sprayed there on the horizon; they seemed dimensionless, like a cityscape in cartoon backdrops. An airplane was coming in toward Idlewild. You could see it but not hear its roar; the city traffic gave it competition.

What Hans might make of all this, she didn't know. She glanced sideways at him. His eyes were open, but it wasn't clear to her he was actually looking, or even seeing. Maybe he was just feeling the daylight on his face. How delicate and even girlish his eyelashes were. His eyebrows so fair they were almost invisible in the strong sun.

"Laura, Laura, are you choosing today to have one of your fits of pique?" called Mary Bernice. "Get down here and help me struggle with these eels before I throw them out in the gutter and lose my job."

"This house is never crazy, till today," said Laura to Hans. "I have to go help her."

"I'm bringing them up to your tub," called Mary Bernice, "but they've been fed on oxblood or something; they're eighty pounds each."

Mary Bernice had been born with a bad hip and she was pint-size to boot: not a midget, as she always said, but the very tiniest giant there ever was. She couldn't manage to carry anything heavy up three or four flights of stairs, and Laura couldn't imagine why she thought she was bringing them upstairs anyway.

"Are you out of your mind?" she yelled. This time she didn't even signal to Hans to stay still and hide—either he had gotten the point by now or it was time to see what would happen if he hadn't. But she closed her door firmly and dashed down, two steps at a time, to where Mary Bernice was struggling with a flat wooden crate lined with plastic. She had gotten as far as the landing on the flight from the front hall. "Where do you think you're going with these?" she asked.

"Grab one end of this before I give myself the heart attack I've always deserved," huffed the cook.

"These don't come upstairs," said Laura. "What are you thinking?"

"Don't give me guff. Aren't I just after returning from the shop when I hear this knock on the utility door. The fishmonger's, and not expected till after lunch today, but their truck busts a gadget and goes out of commission, so they have to do the East Side deliveries early. What am I supposed to say? If your grandmother were here we could pack them in the salt to kill them at once, but I've never done it on my own and if I ruin them Mrs. C. will pack *me* in salt. So we have to keep them alive till she gets home and she can put them out of their misery."

"But where are you bringing them?"

Mary Bernice lodged a hip against a chair rail at the base of the next flight. "The laundry sink has split a seam, don't you know, and the water gushes out fast as you can fill it. Would go all over the laundry floor if you let it. I can't have this mess of eels dying in the kitchen sink, not when I've forty-five chores to do in the next hour. The only place is your tub, Laura."

"You're not putting filthy fresh eels in my *tub*!"

"You think I dare put it in your grandmother's lavatory? You've already had your bath, I heard the water run for an hour. It's just till your nonna comes back from the beauty station. These eels won't bother anyone. They can't get out."

"Why can't she cook with tinned eels like everyone else?"

"A certain Mr. Corm Kennedy, do I need to spell it out for you again? She wants everything the most sumptuous that money can buy. Every fresh ingredient, no expense spared. Watch the corner of that banister, you don't want to dump these fresh gals out all over the carpet. Your folks would have to put the house on the market."

The more Laura protested, the longer it would take. She gritted her teeth and together they heaved the box to the top floor. Don't come out, Hans, thought Laura, don't come out. You'll send Mary Bernice into conniption fits.

They balanced the wooden crate on the edge of the clawfoot. Mary Bernice turned on the taps. "Rosa Mendoza's been avoiding her scouring duties up here, I see," said Mary Bernice, looking at the state of the tub. "I'll have a word with her before she gets sacked. Disgraceful. But it won't hurt the eels none. In you go, ladies." The water having reached a good eight inches, Mary Bernice cracked open one end of the crate with the screwdriver she kept in the kitchen for knocking sense into sticky jar lids. She and Laura tilted the box. It said AMERICAN ILLS in hand-scrawled block letters on the side. Three eels and a slush of melting packing ice slipped out. Released, the eels writhed like octopus tentacles, like live black stockings, slipping in and out and around one another with a sensuous, desperate, evil intensity. It was hard to settle each one as single; they were like the snakes on Medusa's head. Two of them a foot long, and one a foot and a half, maybe. The smell was Baltic.

"You've got yourself dolled up for helping in the kitchen," said Mary Bernice drily, pausing for breath with her hand on the towel rack. "You can bloody well go change into some clamdiggers and an old jersey, you can, for we have work to do."

"This dress has a stain on the sash so it's not an outdoor dress anymore," said Laura. "I'll be down in a little while."

Garibaldi was in the hall, sniffing first at Laura's door and then stalking the perimeter of the bathroom. "The old devil himself," said Mary Bernice fondly.

"No, m'dear, you're not getting your claws into these eels, or else your granny will get her claws into me, and then where would we be?" She closed the door to Laura's bathroom firmly and shooed the cat ahead of her down the stairs. "This may be a school holiday but it's no picnic," said the cook. "Slide your feet into some flats and hurry down. We have to scrub the mushrooms to get ready for all them unhealthy spices and vinegar she drowns them in, and then there's leeks that want rinsing, and the plum tomatoes, and don't get me started."

When Mary Bernice had traipsed down the stairs, leaving the box by the tub for hauling the eels back down to the kitchen when called for, Laura ducked into her bedroom. "I'm going to go get your clothes into the dryer and we'll have you decent in no time," she told Hans. He was prowling around her room, opening her dresser drawers. He must be bored. "We'll figure it out," she said. "Miss Parsley says we all have to rescue ourselves. Just be quiet and stay here, and eat something. Please? I'll be back as soon as I can. Here's a couple of *Teen* magazines you can look at. On my dresser, see? And my old reader from English class, which I forgot to give back. It has some pretty good stories in it." It didn't really, but she had nothing much else to offer. He raised a wing without turning around, as if signaling that he heard her. She guessed he must be bored. She couldn't blame him.

She closed the door once more and launched herself downstairs, two steps at a time, the way she did in Driscoll if she was running late for a class. Flashing through the front hall, she saw the lads going out the door. "See you later, alligator," said Sam.

"Wait?" she asked, and Sam waited in the open doorway, all the cold of a New York December flooding in around him, crisp, coniferous, and diesel. "The owl," she said. "The baby."

"She wants out," he said. "Who don't?"

"What are you going to do?"

"She's starting to bash her wings against the overturned milk crate I got her in. She's about to hurt herself."

"Why don't you let her fly around your place?"

"Would, but I worry about Mittens."

"Who?"

"My mama's pet snake. Now, when I can, I'll let Fluster go. I'll take her to Central Park at nighttime, maybe tonight, maybe tomorrow night. She find her mama, or some juicy mouse out for a midnight stroll, I dunno. But I'm not doing Fluster any good anymore by keeping her. Don't want her to hex me. I got enough hex already." He lifted his chin. "You want to come with me when I let her go?"

"They'd never let me do that," she said.

"She's in her box, you in yours," replied Sam. "Same thing. See you tomorrow."

"Little chinwag with the locals," observed Mary Bernice when she had clattered down to the kitchen. "Your grandmother would have some opinions about that."

"I'm a local, too, you know. I live here. For now."

"So do these vegetables until they get served up tomorrow night. Can you start by rinsing the lot of them? Then lay them on a towel on the drainboard."

"I have to move over the wash first." She scurried into the laundry room, an airless chamber fitted out with venting for the exhaust. She lifted the washing machine lid and pulled out hanks of rotted material, more like seaweed than items of clothing. The fabric came apart in her hands, one gloppy fistful after another. "Crap," she muttered, such an unholy word for the Advent season, but she had run out of holy words several days ago. She clawed out the washer and dumped the mess in one of Mary Bernice's aprons. This she rolled up like a parcel destined for the laundry, tying it with the apron strings, and she bundled it out the back door into a trash can. She'd have to make a new plan. Hans couldn't spend the rest of his life in Nonno's bathrobe.

She was halfway through the vegetables, lost in her own thoughts, while Mary Bernice cleaned the shrimp with a paring knife and hummed "Silent Night" so slowly it sounded like a dirge, when they heard Nonna's foot on the stairs. She came down the flight of steps slowly, cautiously. "*Eccola, la nuova donna,*" she said when she finally appeared in the doorway.

"Holy Mother of God," said Mary Bernice. Laura looked up.

Nonna stood with her arms outstretched. "Very in fashion?" she said brightly, nervously. "Today's beauty?"

She meant her hair. Some sorceress had waved a wand and replaced Nonna's grey heap of pompadour with a shiny black military helmet. The hairdo was stoic and cruel on her head, and looked hard as boiled candy. It made Nonna's face more lined than ever. "It isn't too much, do you think?"

"Any more and you'd need the services of an undertaker," muttered Mary Bernice. "I mean that in a mostly pleasant way."

"It's—it's—whatever were you thinking of?" asked Laura, buying time.

"Tell me you like it, that's what I came for," snapped Nonna.

"I think it'll scare the owls back into the ceiling," said Mary Bernice. "And that's a good thing."

"I love it," said Laura insincerely. "Especially how it seems so stiff and unnatural."

"It's the latest style, that's what Miss Agnes tells me. A sort of understated Jackie Kennedy without the flip. It wants a pillbox to complete it but I would look like a walking bottle of aspirin if I put a little cloth cap on top of my head."

"Really," said Laura. "It's not so bad. We're just surprised."

"Startled," said Mary Bernice, "into silent rapture, no less."

"Not quite silent enough," said Nonna. Then she reached to her forehead and pulled off her hair. Laura let out a soft scream. "It's a wig, *carissima.*" But underneath the wig Nonna's hair had been shorn to make her look like a general from the armed forces, or a mother superior whose wimple had blown off in a gale. "I'm going to put this hairpiece on your dresser, Mary Bernice, if you don't mind. And we'll keep Garibaldi out of your room lest he get ideas."

"Cozying up to a pelt," whispered Mary Bernice to

Laura as Nonna headed into the half-size bedroom. "Being a house cat, Garibaldi might take that wig for a kind of Times Square floozy, I bet. A pussycat from outer space."

"Mary Bernice!" Laura whispered back.

"What can I tell you, he's an Italian cat."

Nonna returned. Her marine crew cut glistened in the overhead light, and you could see liver spots on her very scalp. "It'll grow out," she said grimly.

So she knew.

She began mixing up the dough for the pasta while Mary Bernice finished deveining the shrimp and Laura diced carrots. "We won't even begin on the spumoni until we're done with onions and garlic and anything to do with fish, and we've hosed the kitchen down," announced Nonna. "Ice cream picks up neighbor flavor."

They worked companionably enough in silence. With short hair, Nonna resembled her husband a lot more than Laura might have guessed. Her hips might be stiff and her breath short when it came to stairs, but her wrists and fingers had lost none of their snap. She had the *impasto per pasta* done up in moments and set aside to rest. "Oh, and the eels arrived, can you credit it?" reported Mary Bernice.

"That's a blessing. We can get them salted and work the slime off. Where did you park them?"

"Laura's bathtub."

Nonna raised her eyebrows, which were now bushier than her hairline.

"What else was I to do, I ask you, with the laundry sink sprung a leak the *Titanic* could admire?"

"I can't possibly manage those stairs and Nonno's contractors have left for the day, so they're no help. You'll have to go fetch them down."

"I'll get them," said Laura hastily.

"You can manage them wriggly nasties?" asked the cook. "Bring some towels or a couple of oven mitts so you don't have to touch them. They'd raise the flesh on a six-day corpse, they would."

"Grab them at the neck, because they can bite, like snakes," said Nonna.

"That's all they are, neck," said Mary Bernice.

Laura did as she was told, hustling upstairs in her silly rustling skirts—Mary Bernice was right, what was she thinking, on a day of chores like this?—and trying to figure out how to clothe Hans while she was at it. Up three flights from the kitchen to the grandparents' floor, and then the steep final stairs to the top floor. She was huffing by the time she arrived.

The boost of energy needed to mount the steps must have broken a logjam in her brain. Of course. There were *two suitcases of clothes* in the crawl space behind the chimney. Marco's clothes. Weeping his head off, Nonno had carried them upstairs himself, five years ago, and slotted them into the shadowy aperture. Unwilling to throw them out, unwilling to give them away, unwilling to look at them ever again. His darling grandson.

"I have a plan," said Laura in a carrying whisper. She could hear it in the echoey hallway, as this upper floor was bare of carpets, except for the pale dingy flop rug next to the bathtub.

Her door was open, and so was the bathroom door, and Hans was standing there. She could feel it almost before she turned the corner to see it. The room was spattered with blood. The swan-boy had bitten through the neck of one of the shorter eels. He was pulling strips of flesh from the slimy black skin. Blood dripped from his mouth, his hands, back into the tub—making it a blood bath, literally.

19

She felt she was seeing—an image too deep to emerge in any tell—the forearms of her brother swimming for Old Saybrook, where the wreck of the small plane had washed up. Reaching, blooded, out to claw at the rocky shore. Though Hans had only one forearm, of course, unlike Marco.

She retched a dollop of breakfast into her hand, and managed to make it the three feet to the toilet bowl before her gorge geysered up again. She used her finger to clear out the scum of cereal from behind her teeth, and wiped the back of her hand on her nose, and her eyes. She flushed the toilet, she stood and rinsed her hands and her mouth, all the while keeping her eyes directly in front of her—no mirror, no sidelong glance.

Her heart seemed to be a hammering on metal, rough menace in her ears.

"What are you doing?" she asked, when she could manage words.

"Hungry," he said. "Eating."

"Pick up those other two and put them in the box," she ordered him, and he did, with his bare hand. She had to slap the lid on to keep the eels from rising up like serpents. "I will have your clothes later today," she continued in a trembling voice. "I will get them. I have work to do now. I know this is hard. We have to figure it out together."

When have I ever figured anything out at all, let alone together with someone, she asked herself, and would have slammed the bathroom door behind her as she left, except her arms were full of eels.

20

The rest of the morning spun by like the world seen from a horse on the Central Park carousel—the same things over and over, the replay that just wouldn't settle down. The sink, the oven, the pantry, the table. Back and forth. The washing up, the rinsing the sink, the boiling of water, the smell of eels growing stronger. They were salted now, gently dying in an old white enamel laundry tub of Nonna's that dated back to the Fall of Rome. Their death reek reminded Laura of the smell that the swan-boy had blown in with. She kept thinking that Hans might come downstairs and scare the hell out of Nonna and Mary Bernice, and then at least it would be a family problem, not just hers. Mary Bernice would get the hiccups and pass out. But Nonna would roll up her sleeves and grab the rolling pin she'd used on the pasta dough. Laura almost wished Hans would show up so she could watch what happened. But of course he didn't.

And he wasn't a foe, he wasn't a threat. He hadn't come to her on purpose. He had no—what was the word the school counselor always used—he had no *agenda.* He just needed to get to wherever he was going without causing World War III around here.

Decant the capers and smush them with the blade of the cleaver. Chop up the fresh thyme and toss it in simmering tomatoes and onions. Go upstairs and bring down the napkins we'll use tomorrow night. No, not the blue ones, go back—the red ones. No, the other red ones, these are the stained everyday ones. I'll do it myself. Yes, these ones. Put them in the washing machine and set it on low. Single rinse, cold wash—we're not made of money. Will ye be wantin' the bloody silver polished, Mrs. C.? (Mary Bernice got more and more Oirish the more overworked she felt.)

They paused for lunch, some improvised bruschetta made with the heel of a loaf of Bavarian rye and the remains of three poppyseed bagels. Washed down with a glass of beer for Nonna and another one for Mary Bernice, and a glass of milk for Laura.

Nonna sent Laura upstairs to the closet in the master bedroom to see if the better tablecloth was hanging there alongside the other dry cleaning, because the tablecloth didn't seem to be in the dining room sideboard where it lived usually. Laura took advantage of the mission and hurried up one flight more to her own floor. Peeking in the door of the bathroom, she saw the head and skin and mess, all that was left of the eviscerated eel. Hans had made some effort to wrap it in a striped beach towel. He'd wiped his hands—his hand—on it—a bloody handprint—and then apparently he'd figured out how to work the taps enough to rinse his hand. A rim of dried watery blood spots circled the bowl halfway up.

She next peered into her bedroom. Hans was asleep on his back, with Nonno's bathrobe open almost to his waist. He sure wasn't Italian; his chest was more marble than mossy. Rock-ribbed but downright doeskin. His arm was flung over his eyes and forehead, and his wing trailed like something broken off the side of the bed. She almost stepped on it as she came closer to make sure he was still breathing. He was.

Of course he was in a coma of exhaustion. How far had he come, she couldn't say. It wasn't just distance, across the heaving cold Atlantic, from some country where they spoke their native tongue in that curt, aggressive gargle. He'd come also, maybe, across time. For the story of the Wild Swans was one of the old ones.

Even the book where Laura had found it was distinguished by a smell of mildew. Its stories were printed on yellowing pages in two close columns of very small print. Etchings showed the figures in the tales being old-fashioned. Wearing loose peasant clothes, like the ones Hans had arrived in. No wonder they fell apart in the wash. Maybe they were a hundred years old.

Where was he going that he hadn't yet gotten to? Her life was only a stopping point for him, she was sure.

She found the missing tablecloth and brought it downstairs, flapping in its transparent plastic envelope. Back to work they got.

About four o'clock they paused. The eels had given up their eel-ghosts and stopped wriggling in their tub; Garibaldi had wanted to get at them so badly that Mary Bernice had had to lock him in the laundry. Now the cook made herself a cup of tea, and a cup of hot chocolate for Laura. For Mrs. C. she arranged to reheat some coffee and add a small, restorative glass of Galliano on the side. The snow had begun again, but in an insincere and even insulting way; it spat against the kitchen windows. The falling dark seemed devoid of joy. Not even the tinny radio offering a program of holiday carols could lift their spirits, and Nonna reached over and turned it off.

"How long have you been doing this supper, Nonna?" asked Laura. "Did your parents put on such a feast back in the old country?"

"Ah, the old country." Nonna slipped off her shoes and maneuvered her feet up on the seat of the extra chair. The overhead kitchen light took on a laboratory intensity, thanks to the undrawn shades and the dark outside the window-glass. In her shorn state Nonna resembled a prison matron. "Back in those broke-tooth days, who had the means to offer even one fish on Christmas Eve? Not us, *cara mia.* But for weeks we saved all our bread crumbs in a clay pot, so we could scatter the tablecloth with them. Waiting until people were walking to church at midnight past our house, my mama would flap the tablecloth out the window in the moonlight, making the crumbs sparkle like this damn snow, to prove we had so much to serve we couldn't even finish the crumbs. My papa would steal used wine bottles from the back of the tavern all through Advent, so he could put empty wine bottles out on the doorstep on Christmas Eve. What a table we must have set, said the wine bottles. No no no my dear, I never heard of such a feast where I come from in Italy. I don't know if anyone does such a thing there. Feast of seven fishes, oh, maybe an American gesture of lotsa-lotsa, you know what I mean? *Abbondanza.* Plenty. I'm tired, the

English, it gives out. We had no new clothes, too little food, we didn't even have paper, when we wanted to send letters to your great-uncle in jail, we wrote them on oak leaves."

"Why is he in jail?" asked Laura.

"He is not still there, you silly child. He died in the early 1930s. He was my brother, do you get this? I saw him before we left Italy in June of 1929. I brought him a lemon and two spoons of honey in a little porcelain cheese dish. He was a thief, of course. Like anyone poor enough, why else would they steal? What else can you do when you need to eat and no one will pay you to pick fruit or olives? You pick for yourself and you eat."

"It's a sorry life, and too much like what I left behind in County Tyrone," intoned Mary Bernice. No one paid her any attention.

Laura stifled a yawn. "It's ridiculous," she said, "to go from scrounging bread crumbs in Italy to killing seven kinds of American fish for one meal."

"It isn't ridiculous to survive," said Nonna, drawing herself up and looking like a bald eagle—especially the bald part. "Something plays a part in survival, something you don't understand. *Omertà,* the men call it. Honor, says the military. Grace, says the priest. What do the women call it?"

That wasn't rhetorical; she was waiting to have the

question returned to her. "What *do* the women call it?" asked Laura.

"Despair," said Nonna. "Despair can be stronger than faith or hope. When you have no faith and no hope, something else mounts up in you. It's just—animal anger. I mean when all the other blessings fail you, the animal sense of desperation uses you. It stands you up and walks you across the room and puts you on a boat and gets you to America. And in America it finds a new name, and that name is—"

"Greed?" supplied Mary Bernice.

"Big, proud pride," said Nonna, clapping her hands. "Seven goddamn fish, one for every day of the week, all at once. And a nice bottle of Asti Spumante from Signore Martini and Signore Rossi, to spit in the eye of bad fortune. Anger and love, same thing: they tell you: you serve this food and prove you survive."

By the end of the day the three generations of kitchen magician had finished the prep for the next evening's feast. The sea-green and yellow circles on the flared dress Laura had chosen that morning were now spotted with tomato sauce, as if the whole outfit had contracted a case of the measles.

Nonno came home and ventured kitchenward to supervise. He had a cardboard box of delicacies—a jar of caponata, two tins of sardines in olive oil, some extra virgin olive oil—"How anything can qualify for being extra virgin is a puzzle the Irish don't know how to solve," observed Mary Bernice. "Nor do we want to."

"*Profumato del paradiso,*" said Nonno, raising two fingers in the air at the steam of pasta water, the sweet simmer of chopped tomato. "Worth every aching hour on the shop floor today to come home to heaven."

"How were the takings?" Nonna, straight to the jugular as usual.

He looked at her with unblinking regard, at that shorn grey head and the pouchy eyes. It was a healthy what-the-hell, or it was a compliment to her inner virtue, that he didn't mention the assault on her scalp, that he didn't shriek and fall on the floor. "Very healthy cash box. Possible best day in ten years," he replied. "I hear two fine ladies from Park Avenue, they looking at bottles of poached fruit in brandy. One lady say, 'This bottle, he charge nearly twice for this as for other one, so get this. It must be better. Better costs. You pay for quality, honey.' "

"We won't be talking about cash flow and the bottom line tomorrow night, Ovid," Nonna reminded him.

"No, but it don't hurt to pack your confidence in your back pocket with your billfold. Is too late to get some supper around here?"

"I can whistle up some scrambled eggs and some garlic toast," said Mary Bernice.

"Do you mind if I just take a plate upstairs tonight?" asked Laura. This wasn't generally allowed, but she had put in her time all day, and anyway she could see that Nonno and Nonna wanted to talk strategy. For once, nobody protested, so Laura made two big sandwiches of peanut butter and Fluff and grabbed some almond biscotti. She poured two glasses of milk without thinking about it, and when Mary Bernice raised her eyebrow, Laura blushed and said, "It's too far down to come for seconds, and peanut butter always sticks to the roof of my mouth."

I have to get some control over myself, she thought, heading out of the room. They're going screwball over needing to cram so much good food into Mr. Corm Kennedy and Zia Geneva. Their livelihoods depend on the outcome. The whole house is shaky.

But as she was trudging upstairs, she wondered who she thought she was fooling. If Hans wouldn't eat Maypo, why would she have any more luck with peanut butter? He was a northern boy—she'd been way wide of the mark to offer him lasagne. What did people from his part of the world eat? Sno-cones? She didn't know where his story origins really were—Sweden, or Holland maybe. He reminded her of a more grown-up version of the boy in the Walt Disney program she'd seen a year ago, maybe, that Hans Brinker on his ice skates. Fleeing down the frozen river. Her swan-boy wasn't from sunny Napoli, but from some snow globe world somewhere. He probably ate ice cubes. As well as eels.

Hans took up at the sandwiches with a glum regard, and even pressed a finger upon the top piece of bread, but at the spongy resistance he recoiled.

He must have slept most of the day. He seemed somewhat stronger. The dreadful eel had restored him. Now that his color was better, Laura realized that when he'd arrived, he'd been pale as hoarfrost. "Are you my sister?"

"I'm not your sister," she said, very softly.

"Will you sister me?"

It was possible for a man to father someone—to make some woman pregnant. And any nice lady could mother some crying kid. But Laura had never heard the word *sister* used as an action before. Nor did she want him to brother her—no no no no, not at all. The one thing she knew was that her brother Marco was dead, and nobody could ever take his place.

"Eat the damn sandwiches or don't eat them," she said. "I'm going to rinse out the bathtub and then have myself a soak."

21

It took four or five good go-rounds to clear the tub of any stink or stain of eel. Laura dumped several big splashes of Mr. Bubble into the thunderous cataract from the faucet, which built up a Catskill mountain range of suds. She locked the door and took off her clothes and sank down till her chin was grazed by peninsulas of foam. She lay in the tub for a long time, not so much thinking as floating.

There was once a girl whose brother had died in a plane crash. Because his body was lost at sea and had never washed up on any shore, she lived in the dreadful hope that he might someday drop into her life again. The hope was dreadful because it was a lie, but it still lay upon her like a

millstone around her neck. She couldn't move. She couldn't hardly breathe.

Laura didn't know what a millstone was but it didn't sound like fun.

The problem with a tell like this one was that there was no place for it to go. She could never say that one day the brother came back. One day he *didn't* come back, and also the next day he didn't come back, and the next day, and the next. Nothing ever happened next.

Still—it seemed so urgent to try. She never got beyond the start of things. One day she might. One day when she was ninety-five. What else could happen in a tell except stating things as they were?

One night during a fierce snowstorm, a boy with one wing of a swan was shipwrecked onto the roof outside of her attic bedroom. The girl rescued the castaway and took care of him. He wasn't her brother, but he was the next best thing—a boy in need. She was nearly not scared of him at all.

Well, that was something, but that was as far as it went. She topped up the hot water and lay, glazed and half asleep, in the greasy slick of expired bubbles.

Finally she rallied. She could hear Hans moving

around the room. She had no idea how much longer she could keep him here, and why she should bother. Sooner or later she would have to get him out and away. But it was too much like the story of her brother—there was no *next* to be able to imagine for him. Who wanted a broken brother who could neither swim nor fly? The only thing a broken brother could do was drown.

Still. Somewhere Hans had a sister who had been able to bring him mostly back from the curse of being a swan. Laura, who had become an only child two-thirds through her life so far, could sister *that* sister. From a distance of an ocean and a century. Laura could try to finish the job somehow. She couldn't weave a cloth out of some enchanted flax and throw a cobbled-together loose sleeve over his swan wing before the year ended. (There were only nine days left to the year, and she didn't even know how to sew, much less weave.) She couldn't turn the boy part of Hans back into a swan, either—where was the magic to do that? She just had to help him get away from here.

She just had to help him get away from her.

That line wasn't what she had thought, but it edited itself in her head. She yanked the plug on its beaded chain, and the bathwater gargled into the pipes.

She had to get dressed again in her puffy dress just to be decent while she retrieved her nightclothes from her bedroom. She left off her bra and her tights because she'd be changing out of them shortly anyway. Once in the bedroom, she found Hans at the window, sitting on the sill and leaning out, holding on to the window frame with his hand and angling his face to the Manhattan sky. He batted his wing with minute adjustments to help him maintain his balance. "What are you doing?" she barked in a throttled voice.

"I don't know," he said. "Looking up, looking down."

The bathrobe had rucked high up upon his thighs. "Get in here before you fall," she snapped at him.

"You *do* sound like a sister," he replied, which almost made her vision zigzag with tears. But she slammed her dresser drawers instead, and she kept her head turned so he could inch back into the room without exposing himself to her.

"I am getting something for you. Stay here," she said.

"Forever?"

"For now."

She went to the crawl space behind the chimney and pulled out the two suitcases. She dragged them to her room and heaved them onto her bed. The buttons to open the latches were stuck, but they sprang open with a little more application of force.

To come upon the clothes of someone who has died five years earlier is to imagine a naked ghost out there somewhere. The clothes still smelled of Marco somehow, but also of dust and time. Laura drove herself forward, through more kinds of resistance than she could name. She was ruthless in her campaign. She located some boxers and some socks and a pair of creased black denim trousers with very tight legs. She found a white T-shirt and a baby-blue button-down shirt. There were no shoes in either suitcase. "Can you get dressed in these?" she asked.

He looked at the clothes with a certain amount of confusion. They didn't look like the outfit of a figure from a fairy tale. They looked like the boys who used to hang around at the soda fountain near 67th and Lexington or underneath the old elevated train on Third. "Come on," she said impatiently, "we haven't got all night."

"Are we going somewhere?" he asked.

"Yes. As soon as we figure out where," she replied, "and how."

He picked up the boxer shorts. He could tell what they were. He dropped them on the floor and stepped in the leg-hole of one, and leaned down to pinch the waistband at the right side. Then his left foot fumbled for the other leg-hole. Laura stooped and guided his foot. She let him hoist the shorts up under the bathrobe. He ran his hand back and forth under the elastic, making the boxers hang straight.

The trousers were more difficult and more intimate. Because the cut featured such a narrow leg, Hans couldn't put them on by himself. Laura turned her head toward the hallway as she helped him draw up the slacks. Since he seemed not to know how a zipper worked, she held her breath and guided his hand to the zipper pull. She showed him how to tug it, and she pulled the fabric in the front of the trousers on both sides so the fastener could rise. Then she snapped the metal rivet for him and breathed out. The punch of the trouser snap was so loud in Laura's ears that she was surprised her grandparents couldn't hear it all the way down in the kitchen, where they were probably finishing their eggs.

Hans let the bathrobe drop—he did, then, have some sense of modesty. She didn't know much more about boys than she knew about swans, when it came to propriety, but she had seen boys in bathing suits before, so his naked chest wasn't very shocking. Flying, if flying he had done, had been good for his pectoral muscles, a term of biology she remembered from Frobisher's week on Human Musculature.

The T-shirt was a problem, but Laura solved it. With her nail scissors she snipped the seam on the left side of the torso from the waistline to the sleeve join, and then across to the hem of the left sleeve. Starting again on the left side of the collar, she scissored from the neck hole through to the top side of the sleeve's hem. Now the T-shirt opened on one side like—

Like a book

Together Hans and Laura wrestled the ripped T-shirt over his right arm and his head, and as for clasping the torn sides together with some kind of button—it just wasn't possible. Laura drew the sash from Nonno's bathrobe through a belt loop under the wing, and tied it over the opposite shoulder. The snug fit of the cord more or less kept the flapping T-shirt from falling off.

She stood back. To dress someone, it was a different kind of tell. "Did you fly here on some artificial wing?" she asked him.

He pouted and shrugged. In that throwaway, insouciant expression he looked American modern, a boy from the CYO dance, a boy on the street with his chums. It was the clothes, mostly, but it was also the disaffected, casual look of kids in charge. Maxine Sugargarten often flashed the female version of that look.

"Could we make you a replacement wing?" she asked him. He turned his head and studied her sideways with the beady scrutiny of a swan readying to raise a wing and beat her to death.

"I can't make anything," he told her, in a voice that suggested she hadn't been paying attention and he hated her for it.

"I can't either. We're made for each other," she said. But as soon as the words were out they sounded flirty, like rough-girl talk.

As if in response, under the lampshade with the caballeros and señoritas dancing across it in sensuous and unbalanced abandon, the forty-watt bulb flickered twice and failed. It made the room appear to go inside out, like a white-and-black negative of a black-and-white photograph. The world in the street seemed to thump itself, cough, and stand up straight. Hans didn't notice, just kept looking at Laura. From below, Mary Bernice, siren to the universe. "Laura? You all right up there?"

"Of course I'm all right," said Laura. "My bulb just blew out."

"The whole street is out. A downed power line. I'll come up with a candle."

"No, don't do that! I don't need one."

"I've known blackouts to last a while. Don't want you falling down the stairs, mind. I'm coming up."

"I'll come down," she called, hearing impatience in her voice. "Stay there!"

"Keep your shirt on," she replied. "Only trying to help."

Laura felt she no longer needed to *shhh* Hans or to give him instructions. He knew the rules of his prison aerie. She felt her way along the hall to the top of the stairs. The mild snowlight marked out the windows, which gave her a sense of the dimensions of the hallways as she descended. Mary Bernice was standing in the front hall just below the repaired ceiling. She had two kitchen candles in wide glass jars, one for her and one for Laura.

"You drop this going upstairs, mind, and you'll burn the house down," she said. "Why don't you stop a while in the kitchen with me and the cat?"

"I'm not scared," she said, "not scared of anything. Are Nonno and Nonna in bed already?"

The key in the front door sounded before Mary Bernice could answer, and in came Nonna with her new hair under a shawl, and Nonno shaking his shoulders and arms the way a duck shakes its wings. "We on our way anyway," said Nonno, "when pouf, someone flip city light switch."

"Panetta's," said Nonna, to Laura's raised eyebrow. "Thought we deserved a little treat after the long day Nonno had, and me, too. We had a glass of wine at the bar and some crostini and olives."

"Two dollar seventy-five," said Nonno, hanging up his coat.

"As Signora Steenhauser says, it's cheap and cheerful, Panetta's," said Nonna. "But you don't want to examine the tablecloths under strong light. Nor the silverware."

"And don't order no scallopini," added Nonno. "We call upstairs to see if you want to come, *cara,* but you run the water, you no hear us."

"That's okay. I wasn't hungry," said Laura. "I'm going back upstairs."

"Help your nonna up steps. So dark, she slip, her new head fall off."

Laura gave Nonna an arm and they inched up two flights, so terribly slowly, until they were at the door to Nonna's bedroom. Nonno was still downstairs, talking with Mary Bernice. "Just get me settled in my chair and wait with me here until Nonno arrives with a candle for us," said Nonna. "I don't like the dark. I sleep with the bathroom light on, which makes Nonno angry, running up the electric bill. But I need a little light."

She settled in the easy chair in the corner of the master bedroom and took off her wig. "What do you think about this, Laura, honestly? Big mistake?"

"Big change."

"I thought I saw Flaviana Zulo, the hat-check girl at Panetta's, stifle a laugh when we came in. I thought she was going to ask me if I wanted to check my hair."

"It's just different." Laura shrugged. "Nothing wrong with different. Your sister will be surprised."

"I haven't seen Geneva since the funeral Mass we had for the soul of Marco," said Nonna. "She doesn't know what I look like these days. She couldn't tell me from Gina Lollobrigida."

Oh yeah? thought Laura. She was eager to get back upstairs to Hans but she couldn't leave her grandmother alone. "We're mostly ready for tomorrow night?"

"Lots more work tomorrow, *carissima.* Mostly setting up. But it's fine. Nonno will be out all day again, and he'll close the store at five. Geneva and her new man are expected at six, and the other guests, too.

We'll have drinks in the parlor while Mary Bernice is arranging the food in the dining room, and we'll come down about seven."

"I'm feeling a little queasy," said Laura, because it was true and also because she wanted to begin to lay down a story about being too ill to join the guests for the Christmas Eve feast of the seven fishes.

"Too bad. Tomorrow you're going to feel well enough to help out all over again," said Nonna. "You're not off the hook, Laura. This investment we need from Mr. Corm Kennedy affects you, too, you know. The convent school isn't cheap. We got the first semester's bill in the mail today. La Société des Plaies Sacrées. I don't quite know what that means but I can guess. The holy wounds."

"I don't want to go to an expensive school. Or any school."

"I don't want to bow down and scrape before my younger sister, either," said Nonna, "but we have to manage somehow. You weren't—what's the word your Mr. G. used—you weren't thriving at school. You didn't have any friends, you weren't getting along. Life is a challenge, Laura Maria Ciardi. You have to meet it."

"Don't get yourself in a state."

"I don't like the dark, I told you. Ah, Nonno."

"*Ecco,* I come bearing light," said Nonno, because

as he crossed the threshold into the room, the light in the bathroom came on. It flickered off and back on again, and stayed on. "I leave candle here because wires, wind, they might be start and stop all night, like last time. Till men in truck come and tie wires together again."

"Good night, Nonno, good night, Nonna."

"Stay a little while, *bambina.* You never come listen to music no more. Let me put record album on hi-fi. You want little Verdi tonight? Little Puccini?"

Laura loved to imagine a little Verdi and a little Puccini standing on the edge of the mantelpiece, discussing the Ciardi marriage. What kind of opera would *that* make? "I want to go to bed, Nonno, I'm tired."

He walked to the portable record player in its houndstooth print case and he moved the newspapers off the lid to open the top. She saw that he was limping a little, favoring one leg. He was getting old, old, and working so hard, and trying so hard to cherish his granddaughter. "Look, the present you got from somebody. Mary Bernice put it here? She think it for Nonna and me. Why not, this room is home for music. Peter, Paul and Maria. Mary." With his fingernail he slit open the paper glued across the mouth and pulled the album out of the sleeve. "We hear little bit, sugar for the ear, one aria, maybe two."

Nonna had leaned back with her plagued head on the bolster and kicked off her shoes. She put her lumpy feet on the ottoman. She closed her eyes. Her face fell into the repose of those who have lost ambition to maintain appearances. "Put on the music, Nonno; we'll dance, or we'll rest and dream that we're dancing, that's better."

The first track was too fast to dance to. Laura was glad, she was sure that Nonno would hate it. But he loosened his tie and undid his vest buttons—he dressed so formally when he was being Signore Ciardi of Ciardi's Fine Foods and Delicacies—and he snapped his fingers like Frank Sinatra, except he missed the beat nearly every time. "Early in morning," he crooned, the only part of the song he could pick up. "Dat's-a da time to shave and get to work, ya bum."

Nonna started laughing. "Give those songbirds a chance to make their point. You're insulting the singers with that stage Eye-talian of yours. Respectable Ovid is losing ground to Vito from the bad streets."

Nonno grinned, took off his white shirt, stained with some kind of brine at the cuffs, and went into the bathroom to find his pills.

"He does love you, Laura," said Nonna in a quiet voice, between the tracks.

Laura couldn't speak, she couldn't move. She thought,

Why does the most obvious thing, the only thing that doesn't need to be said, hurt so much when it is actually said out loud?

"Bella, you send my bathrobe to laundry?" called Nonno. "No here nowhere."

The next track came on. Laura would wait through this one—the songs were quick—and then dart upstairs. It was mostly a solo by the lady singer. She was on a train going one hundred, two hundred, three hundred, four hundred, five hundred miles. Five hundred miles from her home. It was the saddest song Laura had ever heard, sadder than *Lasciatemi morire*, the "Lamento d'Arianna" of Monteverdi that her grandmother favored. *Leave me here to die!* In Peter, Paul and Mary's song, death wasn't even a choice—just separation. Lord I'm one, Lord I'm two, Lord I'm three, Lord I'm four, Lord I'm five hundred miles from my home.

"How far is Montreal from here?" asked Laura.

"Don't ask," said Nonna. Her eyes were wet. "Don't do that to us, Laura."

"I'm guessing it's about five hundred miles."

"Take off the damn record, then."

"You take it off." She called through the bathroom door, now closed, "Ciao, Nonno, good night." She had already kissed her grandmother once and she didn't bother to repeat the gesture. She took her candle and that was a good thing, because as she mounted the flight to her rooms, the electric power stuttered again and the lights went dead. The voice of Mary cut out, probably about three hundred and twenty-five miles from her home.

22

She set the candle on her dresser. An oval wobbled on the ceiling; that was the thicker glass of the edge of the jar. Her room by candlelight. She'd never seen it like this.

He was lying on the bed, on his back. His eyes were closed but his breath was interested; his lungs weren't making the long ellipses of sleep like the ones Miss Gianna Tebaldi had been prone to issuing from her room down the hall. He was intact and alert. With his one hand he had somehow managed to undo the snap of Marco's trousers and they were a swirl of shadow kicked against the baseboard.

She looked at her nightgown on its hook. It hung

there like an old life, like a disguise, like Nonna's new hair—vague, and vaguely repulsive, and redundant.

She took off her dress and draped it neatly across the back of the wicker chair where he had slung the T-shirt and the sash from Nonno's bathrobe. Then she sat on the side of her narrow bed. He didn't inch over to make room and he didn't flinch. Slowly, gingerly she lay back upon his chest, settling her head in the crook between his neck and the curve of shoulder-into-wing. They were both facing the ceiling, the dancing ovals thrown by candlelight. The wind scored the night with long atonal flourishes, *accelerando, fortissimo, ritardando.*

His arm was stretched out, cantilevered like a dead Christ's arm. She threw her right arm out over his. He was only a little taller than she; her hand fell against his wrist and her fingers washed up into the cup of his palm.

She kept her other arm loosely across her breasts. After a while he folded his wing upon her arm and the sensitive tops of her legs, a swan's down blanket beating with his own blood. She thought: His Nordic chill, my Mediterranean sun. His heroic north against my Catholic south. Pagan magic against Christian miracle. Had she not been lying down she might have swooned.

Take good care of my baby.
500 miles, 500 miles, 500 miles, 500 miles.
Leave me here to die.

Dolce, più dolce.

23

As she passed the dining room doorway the next morning, Laura saw two elderly men having breakfast across from one another. Then she realized the second man was Nonna without her new hair. Today she looked like a Roman senator or Caesar, erect, capable, bloodthirsty.

"And now that I've finally got you to myself," said Mary Bernice in the kitchen, fiddling with scorched toast stuck in the gridlines of the device, "may I please be honored with the news of what happened to that third eel?"

"What third eel?"

"You know what third eel. When you bring them down yesterday, there's only a pair of them. What with everything else, the missus didn't notice, but I did."

Laura tried to tell it in her head before she spoke it.

"Oh," said the girl casually, tossing her long beautiful hair, "the cat got it."

"Garibaldi," said Laura.

"Garibaldi never did such a thing in his sainted life."

"Maybe having the little owl in the house awakened Garibaldi's killer instinct."

"That geriatric cat got it out of the *tub*?"

"I found it out of the tub. It flipped out by itself and the cat only mauled it after it was dead? Maybe? You know how they wriggle. I cleaned it up and threw it out. I didn't want to tell you because I know you love that cat."

They both looked at Garibaldi, who was sitting on the windowsill, scrupulously studying the nothing that was going on in the backyard. "Shame on you, you filthy beast," said the cook. "And at holy Christmastide, no less."

"We were going to eat it anyway," said Laura. "And it isn't sacrilegious, because as far as I ever heard, there weren't any eels at the stable worshiping the baby Jesus."

"You're full of beans this morning. Eat up this toast, I haven't got time for oatmeal. We're in the run-up to blessed insanity today, I can just feel it." Mary Bernice stood on the stool to reach the larger colander. She cast a sidelong glance at Laura. "You've been looking peaky this past week. Do you seem a little rosier this morning or are my old Irish eyes playing tricks on me?"

"Your old Irish eyes are blind."

"I know a young girl's fancy. That's an awful nice dress for a day of house chores. And you've put your hair up like bloody Audrey Hepburn. Either you're trying to be *Breakfast at Tiffany's* or you're out to shame your grandmother, which isn't very nice of you, though I get it."

"I want my hair out of the way. I have a lot to do today. If you need my help, can we get started."

"You can start by having your toast. Then we'll rinse the lettuce and go on from there, and see how we get on." She eyed the heap of shaved Parmigiano-Reggiano in a bowl. "I might need to send you out for some cheese reinforcements." She poured a saucer of milk for the cat, purring at it in an Irish accent. "I have another theory."

"About the eel?"

"About Little Miss Fancy. You've cast your eye on that John Greenglass, haven't you."

"Don't be silly. Or rude."

"Oooh, I'm gettin' above me station, am I," said Mary Bernice. "So sue me, sweetheart."

Laura ate a couple of bites of toast and made a show of tossing the rest in the trash. "Feeling our oats," observed Mary Bernice in a drier tone of voice. "Well, I better get the eggs up to your grandparents before they terminate my services on Christmas Eve, and me out in the cold with my nose pressed against the glass." She slung a tray of eggs and small sausages into the dumbwaiter. "You can get a head start on ironing the napkins if you have nothing better to do. Wash your hands first lest you get butter on them."

"How much flatter can napkins be?" asked Laura, but did as she was told.

Standing over the ironing board, she waited for the iron to heat up. That smell of hot starch and slightly scorched soap powder residue. The heft of the iron in her hand. She had new measures for heat and heft this morning. Her whole body was different, her whole self. The world screening itself through her senses had a renewed character.

When Mary Bernice returned to the kitchen, she lit the back burner and put on a big pot. "Potatoes," she said.

"Potatoes, with all this pasta?"

"Potatoes for me and Ted, tomorrow. I won't get home till midnight tonight, the way things are going, and I have his Christmas dinner to get, too, you know. None of this messy Mediterranean menu for Ted. I'm doing a sensible roast with carrots and onions. I already made the Christmas pudding last week with suet I picked up at Frombacher's, and it's getting drunker by the day. This isn't the only household that celebrates Christmas, you know."

"Does Ted mind that you spend so much time here?"

"He likes the pay packet I bring home, and so do I. Could I dare to think you might peel these potatoes if you're done with the napkins?"

"What made you choose Ted?" Laura asked. "Were you always in love with him?"

Mary Bernice wrestled with a five-pound bag of flour. She dumped it in the flour bin of the Napanee, a battered, stand-alone cabinet. "I'm not much of a catch," she said, "four-foot-eleven in my best pumps. And I seem to lack the right factory for being a mother because it's been twenty-some years and never a breath of hope in that department. But Ted is steady, and so am I, and steady likes steady."

"Like isn't love," observed Laura, gouging the eyes out of her victim potato.

"Oh, sweet Jesus of Queens and the Bronx, and parts beyond," said Mary Bernice, "this is a fine time to start dissecting romance. Really, I'm not the right person, but who else will show you sense from nonsense? I'll only say this, my duckie. When you're young, there's a lot of flare in the dark, a lot of struck matches and sparks. They shock and please and they don't last. That's a lot of like and a whole lot of like. Love is something slower to find. It's usually muted and in my experience you are standing right there at the bus stop next to it for a year before you even notice it. That's one Irishwoman's opinion and it doesn't count for much, but Ted and I have been together going on twenty-two years. He has no roving eye and nor do I."

"I think it's you who are stuck on John Greenglass, not me," said Laura.

"Dig your own eyes out with that peeler, why don't you, and let me get on with my work. You've a bit of a mouth on you this morning, Laura. Can't say I mind, but it's damn poor timing. Now shush about all this. Here comes your nonna to beat us with an iron skillet. Throw a towel over them potatoes before I get sacked. We'll get back to them later."

Nonna arrived. Nonno left for the shop. The kitchen was a madhouse for the second day running. At one point Garibaldi escaped out the door to the upstairs, but Laura forgot to worry about that. Twenty minutes later he came streaking downstairs and hid under the pleated skirt of Mary Bernice's rocker. "What's gotten into that maniac?" said Mary Bernice. "He's at Panic

Central like the rest of us, but what's taken him so long, is my question." Laura thought: He's met Hans upstairs, and he's lost his mind, the way I have.

The doorbell rang, and Laura was sent to answer it. John Greenglass and Sam Rescue. "You're not going back upstairs today, I imagine," she told them more than asked them.

"Shouldn't need to," said John, scrutinizing his work on the ground floor. "Looks like the repair is holding. This ceiling has dried, the primer is dry. We'll just roll over a clean coat of white across this ceiling. Be done in a jiffy, and out of here till the next time the building falls down."

"You want to hear about the owl?" asked Sam Rescue.

Laura pivoted at the doorway to the kitchen steps. "Well, yes, of course."

"Took her to Central Park last night. Had to let her go or I'll be watching her kill herself, won't I. I wait till the middle of the night. Bring her in my lunch box. When I get to a wide-open space, nobody around, I sit on a bench and put the lunch box next to me. I open it up, and guess what, she just sits there for about five minutes, looking around at the big ole sky. It was clear, nothing but stars."

"I know," said Laura.

"Then she sort of hop up and kind of fall over onto the bench, and she hop some more, like a pigeon. I din't know owls could hop. She come right up on my leg and squeeze my leg with her little thorny things—"

"Talons," said John, setting up a ladder.

"And she stay there for another couple of minutes. It was getting pretty cold and I din't want to sit there all night, but I din't want to shoo her off, either."

"Steady is steady," said Laura.

"Then she leave, all at once, a big whoosh of feathers and noise in my face, and a little rip in my blue jeans and a bloody scratch I see later when I get home. She fly like a pro, Laura, like she never fell in no house and scrabble down into a damp ceiling. Like she know the whole map of Central Park and she got someplace to go. You know what I think?"

"You think it's time to open the paint and give it a good stir," said John.

"I think I wish I knew the map of the world as good as she does," said Sam. "I can't hardly remember whether it's the GG or the Number Two to get from heaven to hell and back again."

Laura said, "Do you think you would know how to build a wing?"

"A wing of a house?"

"A wing for a—" Laura paused to ask herself what

A wing for an angel, said the girl, with the most honesty ever she spoke.

"—a wing for an angel."

"Why, you break one of your own wings?" asked Sam Rescue, and gave her a wrinkled, wicked little sparkly smile.

"It's—for the church pageant."

Oh, if necessity is the mother of invention, who is the father? Fantasy.

She continued. "The angel, you know, Hark, the herald angel sings? He has two wings, of course, and there were two girls, one to hold each wing. But Donna Flotarde got hit by a bus and she couldn't finish her wing. So could you help me make one?"

"She wasn't hurt bad?"

"Oh, very bad. Sadly, she'll probably live. But that wing?"

"Your grandparents going to pay for the overtime?" asked John Greenglass.

"Hey, Greenglass, I do it on my own time, if I can," said Sam. "We knocking off early today, so Laura, you tell me what you have in mind. You need it by tonight, right, because poor Hark the *Herald Tribune,* he got to sing his song?"

"That's the idea."

"I'll holler for you when we're done with this ceiling, and we'll see what we can jig up."

"You're on your own," said John. "I got to get a last-minute present for my baby." The way he said it, Laura couldn't tell if he meant his girlfriend or his infant child.

Back to the kitchen, back to the rinsing of scallops and the chopping of red peppers and then, yes, by midmorning, a run for more cheese. What was Nonno thinking, only half a pound? There were six guests tonight. But the corner supermarket would have to do; Ciardi's Fine Foods and Delicacies was several blocks farther away.

Before Laura could collect cash from Nonna's purse for the cheese, and while you're at it a quart of heavy cream, the doorbell rang again. "Just like Geneva!" said Nonna, patting her head, as if she hoped her original hair had grown back in since breakfast. "If that is my sister showing up early to shame me in my *stato vestito,* I am going to kill myself," she continued, "and then I will kill her, and let Mr. Corm Kennedy and Nonno fight a duel for the change. Answer the door, Laura, please, and if it happens to be a caller and not someone delivering another godforsaken poinsettia, show them into the waiting room and close the door, and I'll rush up the back stairs and arrange my face."

The idea of Nonna rushing anywhere was a laugh. Laura did as she was told. There were two people at the door. One was a delivery guy with, yes, a poinsettia in a sealed paper envelope like a cone. The big packet of plant blocked the little person slightly behind the delivery guy. Only when Laura had put the flowers down on the floor in the front hall and turned back did she recognize the visitor. If it were a woman Laura couldn't recognize, it might be Zia Geneva, because Laura hadn't seen her great-aunt since Marco's service and couldn't remember her at all. But it was a different relative.

"Oh, we weren't expecting *you*," said Laura, not meaning to be unkind.

"I don't like no telephone, you get voices in your head from the telephone, and we have enough voices in the head already, so I took the early Greyhound," said Nonna di Lorenzo. "I hope you going to ask me in and not just talk to me here on this stoop like I'm sister collecting for Saint Colman's Home for Children."

"Sure, come in," said Laura, and to the lads behind her in the hall, "this is my other grandmother. Signora di Lorenzo."

"*Buongiorno*," said John Greenglass, and to Laura,

"What? You think I haven't picked up any Italian, working here all week?"

Laura installed Nonna di Lorenzo in the waiting room. "I'll get Nonna Ciardi, but it might take her a moment. She's not fully dressed."

"I dressed by five-fifteen in the morning," said Nonna di Lorenzo. "Really, Laura, I came to talk you, mostly, but ask Nonna Ciardi to step in, see me for few moments. She should know about this, very also."

Laura closed the door on Nonna di Lorenzo, a much smaller and frailer old lady than stout Nonna Ciardi. "You got them coming out of the woodwork," said John Greenglass.

"What, more owls?" asked Laura.

"Grandmothers."

Sam muttered, "Don't she look like she could be a grandmother owl herself, though, showing up to find out what ceiling her stupid granddaughter got herself stuck into." He had a point. Nonna di Lorenzo was tiny and bony and her fried hair was short and scattershot, every-which-way, a white feather duster someone had trimmed with nail scissors.

Nonna Ciardi was livid at the news, and at first refused to come upstairs at all.

"It must be important, Nonna. She hasn't been to New York City in a while," said Laura.

"It's only polite to say hello," intoned Mary Bernice.

"When I need my cook's advice on manners I'll fire you and hire another cook," snapped Nonna Ciardi. But she wrapped two tea towels on her head and shucked off her apron. "If she thinks she's getting an invitation to stay over, she's got another thing coming. We haven't time to make up Miss Gianna Tebaldi's room for her, and anyway, that old quail-hen would never manage the top flight of steps."

But by the time Nonna Ciardi and Laura returned to the waiting room, Nonna Ciardi had composed her face and calmed down. "*Se non si credo, non può essere vero.*"

"*Gesù ti aiuterà a portare i tuoi fardelli, mia cara signora.*"

"English, please," said Laura. "The only Italian words I know are swears."

"Santa Lucia, a blessing on Christmas Eve, to see you again!" Nonna Ciardi said to the other grandmother. "It's mayhem around here, Magdelena, but I will sit down with you for a few minutes and find out how you're keeping. Laura, park yourself. The cook will bring us some coffee, Magdelena, if you've time to take some."

"Oh, the *cook,*" said Nonna di Lorenzo, but seemed to think better of starting out shirty. "Isabella, you and your Vito have beauty home."

"*Ovid,*" said Nonna Ciardi pointedly, "is at his shop. He will be sorry to miss you. I suppose you can't stay long."

"It seems no," said Nonna di Lorenzo, looking around and drawing her coat around her. No one had asked her for her wrapper, and she seemed to realize she was getting a brisk reception.

"I don't mean to be rude," said Nonna Ciardi. "We are having guests, Magdelena, and this morning the kitchen is the absolute sacking of Rome." She drew herself up and took a deep breath, and gambled. "We could perhaps pull up another chair at table tonight if you are staying in the city? No?"

"No, no, *devo essere a casa.* I am expected to arrive back in Albany at three. I am on altar guild and have work in church at five. Umberto to meet me at bus terminal and to drive me."

"You've come all the way from Albany for a quick hello?"

"Is more than hello. Is thank you to you and Vito—Signore Ciardi." She seems not to want to call him Ovid, thought Laura. Nonna di Lorenzo went on. "I want to see my Laura, *carissima ragazza figlia del mio cuore.* I need to kiss her and kiss her. I need to tell you both about Renata, and to thank you for your help all these years. I no write good in English or *italiano,* and the telephone bad bad. Bad in itself, bad for bad news. Too far away."

"Is there bad news?" Nonna Ciardi looked about as sentimental as it was possible for a marauding Visigoth to manage. Just then Mary Bernice swung in with a tray of tea things. "I said coffee," barked Nonna Ciardi, but Mary Bernice didn't even reply. Garibaldi stalked in behind the cook and began to bat at low-hanging ornaments on the forlorn Christmas tree in the bay window.

"All these years, you send the dollars, you so kind to us," said Nonna di Lorenzo. "For now, you stop. I need to thank you with my own lips, dear Signore Mrs. Vito Ciardi. Dear Isabella."

"Why, has something happened to Renata?" Nonna Ciardi glanced at Laura, trying to decide whether or not to send her out of the room.

Nonna di Lorenzo pulled the sides of her coat together, as if she were sitting at an icy bus stop. "*Lei ha un ictus, un grumo di sangue.* She lose the strength of her right face. No words, no muscle. They take her into public hospital. They do not think she get good, not ever again." Nonna di Lorenzo looked glassily at Laura. "Your mama, *mia dolce ragazza,* she have the strokes. Her hard life, first her husband Giuseppe, then her beloved boy Marco, all gone. I do my best for her these years, and her soul no good, no good, sick with *grande dolore.* But now it not just her soul, but her mind, her spirit. It broken, she broke, she no walk, no talk, no feed herself. Umberto take me to visit each every day. I afraid she die, I want Laura to know before her mama she die. She at Ann Lee Home on public dollar. She miss you every day, Laura, every hour, every day. She no strength to raise you good, so Nonna Ciardi and Nonno Ciardi, all this years, they have money, they have *enorme simpatia,* they take you in and raise you up."

"But this is dreadful," said Nonna Ciardi. "You must get a second opinion."

"Nobody ask for second opinion from *Gesù,* or get opinion of the devil."

"Don't be a fool, Magdelena. A doctor. Shall I help you line up another doctor?"

"There no time. I want bring Laura back with me to say goodbye."

"I can say goodbye to you here," said Laura.

"Laura, *tua madre, non la rimanga molto tempo in questo mondo.* She do not get good again. She flying home to *Gesù.* You come with me."

"That's out of the question," said Nonna Ciardi, standing up. "Goodbye."

"Nonna!" said Laura, though it *was* out of the question, for so many reasons.

"We are bringing Laura to Montreal in ten days," said Nonna Ciardi, relenting. "Perhaps we can stop in Albany and visit . . . on our way."

"I have already think you say something like this. Only come in time." Nonna di Lorenzo stood up as well. The tea had not been touched, not even poured. "You help me feed Renata all these years. Every two weeks, you send money for food. You send up the *pacchetti di prosciutto crudo.* We do not eat with you no help. That all done now. But why you never come to visit my daughter? In her sadness? She wife of your Marco, mama of your Laura."

"Give my very best to Umberto," said Nonna Ciardi.

"We starve without you help," finished Nonna di Lorenzo. "I throw myself at you feet to say *grazie prego ciao.*" She looked as if she wanted to kill Nonna Ciardi.

"You're sure you can't stay for dinner? We can squeeze you in."

"No squeeze *me.*" Nonna di Lorenzo held out both her hands to Laura, who wanted to do nothing but run away. But Laura went forward and took both the hands of Nonna di Lorenzo. She kissed her mother's mother on both cheeks, and submitted to a dry angry embrace, a pummeling, remonstrative embrace, though nothing was Laura's fault, was it? Nothing. Nothing except that she, Laura, still existed and she still lived while her father, brother, and now mother rushed to the cliff edge of life and plunged over. "You come to me, Laura. Umberto he pick you up at Albany train station or at Trailways depot. I no money, I no schooling, but I no short of love. You only one left when my Renata go to *Gesù.*"

"Merry Christmas, Nonna di Lorenzo," said Laura.

"How is merry, how is happy new year?" She pinched Laura's cheeks. She was smaller than Laura by nearly a head. "My, how you grown so. *Ho bisogno che tu viva. Ho bisogno che tu viva per poter vivere.*"

"Me, too," said Laura, which over the years she had found was usually a safe thing to say to Italians.

Nonna Ciardi escorted Nonna di Lorenzo to the front door. "Did you bring us this nice poinsettia, how kind," said Nonna Ciardi.

"I no bring."

"Then let me give it to you to take away."

"I no take." Then she was at the top step, looking this way and that, and then glancing up in the sky, as if afraid a hawk was going to swoop down and carry her off. Laura called her goodbyes, but Nonna di Lorenzo had finished her work on Van Pruyn Place and did not reply or turn around to wave. She stepped down to the pavement and crossed the street and was lost behind a Westinghouse repair truck.

"Well," said Nonna Ciardi meekly as she made her way down the stairs to the kitchen, "wasn't that a nice surprise."

"What did she mean," asked Laura, following, "you have been sending her money and ham?"

"Nothing. She meant nothing except to try to shame us for not visiting. When all along it is Nonno and me who give you your home. Your other nonna is a strong lady with a terrible life. Like the rest of us, Laura. You will see as you grow older. You would do well to have half her strength. But she's *demente* with sorrow, and that's bad. Sorrow is useless to us. Now you have to go get some more cheese before the doorbell rings and it's Geneva with her man and his big wallet."

Laura said, with some effort, "I often don't understand what is going on, Nonna. Did she say that my mother is sick?"

"Yes," said Nonna briskly. "Sick and maybe dying. What does Nonna di Lorenzo know? She is a *contadina*. But she may be telling the truth. As soon as we can find out how, we will make a plan to visit your mother, Laura. Rennie was never right upstairs, you see, after Marco died. We took care of you to help Rennie try to recover. We never want to alarm her or to make her upset. It is not easy to know the best thing to do, but we do the best we know how."

"Who is Umberto? He's not my grandfather."

"Some parish man, I don't know, some friend from the village back home. Nobody. Don't ask."

Fifteen minutes later, with great relief, Laura was a few blocks away, standing in a long line of frantic, last-minute shoppers. She had two shakers of commercial Parmesan cheese in her shopping basket as well as five lemons and some curly parsley. Garnish and varnish for the plating of it all, as Mary Bernice put it. The market was bedlam. Laura was the twelfth person in line when a cashier returned from her break and flipped her CLOSED sign to OPEN. There was a scramble to switch to the new lane. Laura was pushy but others were pushier, and she was number five in the new line. Right in front of her, turning around as if directed by a mutual spasm of second sight, were Donna Flotarde and Maxine Sugargarten.

24

"Look who's here," said Donna. She had a plastic bottle of Clorox and a small sack of candy canes in her hands.

"Poisoning little children again, I see," said Laura, who couldn't help herself.

"Oh, that's good," said Maxine, whose nose, if possible, was even more thickly bandaged than yesterday. She wasn't carrying groceries, so she must just be kicking around with Donna. "This *is* a surprise, Laura. I was going to come over and see you after shopping. I wanted to tell you something."

"Don't let *me* stop you, Maxine," said Donna. "There's an informational tabloid in this convenient rack. I'll just read this cover story about the alien take-over of the White House. They've brainwashed baby John-John Kennedy. *So* informative."

"You came over yesterday," said Laura to Maxine. "You already said you were sorry I got expelled. I almost believed you. But there's nothing left to say."

The line moved fast as they all pretended to be interested in the racks of Life Savers and Doublemint chewing gum. Donna tore the grocery bag out of the hands of the clerk and said to Maxine and Laura, "I'm expected home, so I'm going home. I hope you're not making a big mistake of *enthusiasm,* Maxine. You'll be sorry."

"Oh, Donna," said Maxine, exhausted. "Mind your own beeswax for once." She loitered as Laura paid for her own groceries. "Sometimes Donna can be so possessive." But Laura didn't want to get pulled into a consideration of the wearying friendship of Donna and Maxine. She had terrible campaigns of her own to manage.

They left the store. Maxine seemed intent on walking Laura home. It was a free country, so why not. They stamped at mounds of slushy snow and inched on icy pavement. Once or twice Maxine started to talk about assignments due over the Christmas break, but Laura finally said, "Don't forget I'm not coming back,

Maxine. Thank you very much. So I don't have to write a damn word about what I did over the Christmas vacation. It's nobody's business but mine."

"Look on the bright side. You don't write very well," said Maxine. "So that's one good thing."

"Now I have to go to school in damned *Canada.*"

That was rich language even for these dire circumstances, and both girls laughed nervously at Laura's street talk. A little while on, Maxine said, "I know I came over yesterday to say I was sorry, Laura. And I am. I didn't know you were going to get expelled. But I didn't steal my own record album and throw it at myself, just for the record. Just for the record, get it?"

"You kill me, Maxine."

"I went to the nose doctor yesterday for a second opinion," said Maxine.

"Opinion about what?"

"My parents didn't want me to go have my nose done," said Maxine. "I've been asking for six months. But the new doctor said I'm probably going to need an operation and as long as they're in there . . ."

"What? As long as they're up your nose?" Laura wasn't quick at cause-and-effect. "I don't know what you mean."

"I'm getting a nose job out of this, Laura. The week after Christmas, the doctor has an opening because all his clients are off to the Florida Keys or to the Bahamas. I'm getting my nose job. I'm so excited. This never would have happened without you."

Even under a bandage like a white felt clamp, Maxine's nose looked perfectly fine. She had that blonde kind of swishy hair that looked great in a high ponytail and also with the right rollers could curl into coils with the circumference of beer bottles. In Laura's opinion, people who already looked Park Avenue had no business trying to look Park Avenue Penthouse. But she didn't care if Maxine wanted to turn herself into Marilyn Monroe. "I'm just saying," said Maxine, "yesterday was *sorry.* Today is *thank you.*"

"Okay. You're welcome. Would you like me to break a couple of your arms next?"

"Oh, Laura. I'm going to miss you, you know. Even if we weren't very nice to you."

"You'll find someone else to bully."

"I wish there was something I could do for you."

They were at Laura's stoop. Van Pruyn Place was a dead end, so it was clear Maxine had no other ambition but to stand here until Laura sent her away. "I wonder," said Laura, "do you know how to sew?"

"I got an A plus in Home Ec," said Maxine. "Didn't you take it?"

"I was doing Remedial Reading that block. Can you sew?"

"Yes, I can sew," said Maxine. "So what do you need sewn? Or should I say, sew what? Get it?"

25

By the time Laura made it through the front door, she could feel anxiety overflowing like a backed-up drain. Mary Bernice and Nonna were raising their voices at each other in the kitchen. The dining room tablecloth was laid, and the candles lined up like white daggers, ready for installation in the fancy silver candelabras. John Greenglass perched on the bottom step of the front hall stairs, writing out a bill for services rendered. Sam Rescue was piling drop cloths by the front door. “We’re going to need one of those,” said Laura, “or maybe two.”

“Drop cloths?” asked Sam. “Your guests such sloppy eaters?”

“For the wing you’re going to help me make. This is Maxine. She’s going to help, too.”

"Smells like fresh paint," said Maxine. "I like fresh paint."

"Whatcha do to your nose?" asked Sam.

"Your grandfather said to leave this bill on his desk," said John. "Can I give it to you to put there, Laura? Sam is clocking off so he can help you some, but I got places to get to, and it's nearly noon."

"Wait here," said Laura to Maxine. Taking the steps two at a time, she raced to the next floor, past the parlor door to Nonno's office. She tossed the folded bit of paper on his desk. Before returning, she stood still for a moment, taking in the air of crisis that bubbled up the stairwells like coffee in the stem of the percolator.

At the root of it, Nonna Ciardi was campaigning to save her husband's business and his reputation. Even Laura could recognize their fear of slipping backward, deeper into the immigrant status they had so laboriously tried to shake, and that Nonna di Lorenzo had not managed, or cared to manage, as well. All that desperate cooking, the pomp and show of food, the fancy linens, the perfect painted ceiling. The effort of it all. It wasn't quite fraud but it was certainly theater.

Up on top, the pacing Hans. Laura could hear him now. He couldn't stay there much longer. If he came downstairs with his torn clothes and his one wing flapping, the world would convulse, and Laura would be sent to live in a home for incurables like her mother. The situation was intolerable, the solution inconceivable. He had to leave the way he came—through the window, with nobody noticing but her. But if he grew desperate and flung himself out, he couldn't escape except by leaping. He would fall, he would die, because who can fly with one wing?

She found herself hurrying upstairs. The door to her room was closed, but when she opened it, she hardly recognized it. Her sheets and coverlet were torn to shreds, and so was Nonno's bathrobe. Wherever he could, Hans was ripping the room apart with his teeth. Her comb, her brush, her framed photo of Marco, had been thrown against the wall. Though the glass in the frame was broken, Marco's face bloomed, undiminished by time or attack or death by drowning. Laura swooped in and picked it up. "What do you think you are doing?" she hissed.

"This is no place to stay, no longer," he said to her. His eyes looked wild and angry.

"You have to be quiet, Hans. You have to calm down." That was what Nonna said to Nonno when his face turned carmine. "I am going to get you out. I am going to make you a second wing so you can fly away."

He swept out his own wing and turned in a circle. He was wearing Marco's trousers but no shirt—the shirt was ripped to shreds, too. The wing was so large Laura had to fall back; it touched three walls of the room as he rotated, and it looked strong enough to beat her down the stairs. "No place for me in this story," he said. For a minute Laura mistook him to mean *on this floor, on this story of your five-story house.*

She tried to arrange her racing mind in its most efficient mode:

For the first time, the young girl was frightened of the strength and power of the swan-boy, and saw him as an intruder in her life, a threat

but while this was clarifying, it wasn't prophetic. That girl in some story in Laura's head didn't know what to do any more than Laura did.

"Your sister made you most of a shirt to make you her brother, make you whole again," she said, "but she failed. So what is left is to let you go back to swan. I don't have any magic but I can try to make a wing and let you go. Where will you go?"

He didn't answer her. No swan knows how to say the map of his ambitions.

Miss Parsley had once told Nonna, at a back-to-school night, that most creative children had active imaginations, but that Laura had a passive imagination. Nonna had repeated this to Laura, hoping to understand the remark, but Laura had felt clueless. Perhaps, now, the way her story-mind had just explained Hans to her without her even trying, perhaps that was what an active imagination was like. Maybe it wasn't to be all gloomy failure for her from now into the distant 1980s by which time she'd probably be dead of old age.

She wished she had the courage of a movie heroine to approach Hans in his wild male panic and to calm him with an embrace, or better yet, a soothing song. All that came to her though was the haunting up-lilt of "500 Miles," and that was a loss-and-longing number, not a courage-in-the-dark-night anthem like the ones preferred by Mr. Ed Sullivan on his TV show.

"You stop this or you'll get me in so much trouble," she said to Hans strictly.

This, it seemed, was enough, or enough for now. He dropped his wing and his chin and he sank on his knees next to her unraveled bed, and buried his face in torn cloth.

"If my plan works, you can leave tonight," she said. "Trust me."

No one had ever trusted her before, and no one should; she had no record of trustworthiness. No history of accomplishment in school or out of it. On the other hand, she didn't have a record of larceny and deceit, either, except for Bobby Vee albums.

She went to the box room and gathered up the ten long thin pieces of wood John Greenglass had called strapping. This was technically stealing, too, no doubt, but she'd have to worry about that later. She managed to get the strips of light wood down the stairs without poking them through the banisters like giant pick-up sticks.

Nonna came up from the kitchen as Laura arrived in the front hall. "*Cosa diamine!* What, this *junk,* why?" she said, nearly screaming.

"Maxine has to make a wing for the Christmas pageant in her church and we're helping her," said Laura. "It's an emergency. Oh, this is Maxine, by the way."

Maxine's poker face was magnificent. She didn't know why Laura was lying and was just fine with it. "Hi, Mrs. Ciardi," she said, unflappable behind her bandages.

Nonna took a look at Maxine's nose and Sam's serene expression and Laura's intensity. Perhaps she did a moral calculation about what was owed to a girl whose nose was broken through Ciardi malfeasance. In any case, she said, "Move into the waiting room. You have one hour and then this goes out in the street. I break it, I burn it myself in the ash can. You hear me, Mr. Roscoe?"

Roscoe? So that was it. Sam Rescue was really Sam Roscoe. It kind of made sense.

"So what's your plan?" asked Sam. Laura said that the wing had to be a little bit longer than her own arm as measured from armpit to palm—maybe three inches longer. It needed three or four thicknesses of strapping for the length, and a roughly triangular armature descending, with the narrowing wingtip at the fingertips. "Obviously," said Sam, and got to work. "I've been watching wings for several nights now." He used small carpet nails and some kind of metal twine to build the skeletal wing-ridge. Meanwhile, Maxine and Laura stretched out the drop cloths. Covered in white plaster dust, drops of white primer and white paint as they were, they looked vaguely feathery already, or like the suggestion of feathers, at least if you squinted your eyes.

Next door in the dining room, Nonna finished setting the candles in their sconces and went up to take a quick bath. Laura prayed, prayed to Jesus Christ and all the saints, that Hans wouldn't be thumping around on the floor above Nonna's rooms. What was a miracle but an enchantment conferred for someone's good? In any case, no shrieks were heard from Nonna. She did not flee from her bath wailing about brigands or beasts in the attic rooms above her.

Downstairs, Laura begged from Mary Bernice the old cookie tin that held needles and yarn, string and scissors, and all manner of sewing implements too vague and surgical for Laura's taste. "You're going to string popcorn for the tree or something?" asked Mary Bernice, tasting the fish broth and wrinkling her nose in displeasure.

"Something," said Laura. "How are things down here?"

"If the pipes don't burst and a ceiling don't collapse and no owls attack us in our beds, we might just get this show on the road and survive the whole thing," replied the cook. "I'll say this for your crazy nonna, she knows how to whip the help into doing what she wants. And she's got a mind like a calculator. We're right on schedule as far as I can tell."

Back in the waiting room, the wing was taking shape. Sam needed some white strips with which to fasten the costume wing to the human arm, so Laura tiptoed upstairs again. Hans was on the floor of her room, looking both furious and exhausted in his sleep. She grabbed most of the torn bedding and trundled it downstairs. The coverlet could give some interior bulk to the wing so it wouldn't look flat like a sailboat sail. And the coverlet, who could have guessed, was stuffed with goose down. As Maxine snipped and stitched to make the coverlet conform, feathers wafted all over the waiting room like snow. Quite a few landed on the Christmas tree. Some leftover grouting compound, thinned with turpentine and dabbed on the wing panel, made a kind of mucilage. Feathers stuck to the fabric. An effort at realism, tawdry but kind of neat.

Nonna came downstairs in her new terrifying hair and a dressing gown over her good clothes. She seemed to be readying to be the placid queen of life around here. "This is a royal mess, this room," she said, "but if we keep the lights off in here except the tree lights, which Geneva and Mr. Corm Kennedy and the other guests can admire from the street, I'll just take everyone upstairs to the parlor for drinks. That was the plan anyway. And why stand on ceremony?" she said, suddenly gay. "If they want to open every door in our home, we have nothing to hide. So we happen to have a teenager at home and there was a last-minute school project. In families, these things happen. This is real life here. Take it or leave it."

"Sorry about all the feathers, Mrs. Ciardi," said Maxine. "That quilt, hoooo-boy."

Laura was afraid to try on the wing and Maxine

wasn't interested, so they tied the white loops onto the right arm of Sam Roscoe, who was about the same size as Hans. He raised the wing and lowered it. When dropped, it pleated in a more or less believable fashion. When raised, it looked strong and also ridiculous, like a joke of a wing. But it looked more strong than it did ridiculous, and that would have to do.

Besides, thought the girl, what miracle didn't look ridiculous while it was happening? If a miracle looked ordinary it would be like, just, so what?

26

Maxine stayed a good part of the afternoon. She got the idea to try to sew some of the goose feathers onto the wing to make it look even more three-dimensional. "I still can't figure out why you need only one wing," she said to Laura.

"I told you, someone else is going to be holding the other wing."

"And why you told your grandmother it was me who needed this."

Laura shot her a look of gratitude for her collusion in the lie, but didn't reply further. She wasn't going to ask Maxine why she arranged an ambush of Laura in the shower, she wasn't going to tell Maxine why she had needed an alibi. Too much truth got in the way.

Maxine grabbed her coat at last. She was going to see Hayley Mills, something just out called *In Search of the Castaways.* The Sugargarten family apparently didn't do Mass and possibly they didn't even do church. Beyond that level of social mystery Laura felt it improper to inquire.

Nonno slumped into the front hall, peeling off his gloves, swiping his heels on the sisal mat. It was snowing out again—just for a change. "You still here," said Nonno to Sam, a little gruffly.

"Was helping Miss Laura with a project. Just about done now."

"Well, you take yourself off. Company coming, got to get ready."

"You bet, Mr. C. Be back after Christmas to tackle the new wall in your bedroom."

"If we still have house," said Nonno, "we fix bedroom. If not, we sleep in Bryant Park with other bums."

Laura didn't want to bring the wing upstairs in case Hans was tempted to try to fly away in daylight. All of New York City's finest would be swarming the neighborhood with police cars and alarms if a young man with wings was seen perching on the top of a brownstone, even in a dead-end street. She followed Nonno up to his room, where Nonna was putting the finishing touches of her makeup on, and choosing among earrings. "Ovid," said Nonna, "are these too Miss Elizabeth Taylor in *Cleopatra*?"

"Who knows what is that?"

"The movie coming out next year, they've been releasing all the photos already. I saw them in a magazine at the hairdresser yesterday. You've seen them, too. She looks like she should be hanging in the window of Baumann's Lighting Fixtures. Do these make me look too much like a tomato?"

"You can't look tomato, you Hope Diamond."

"What do you think, Laura?"

Laura thought that Nonna looked more like Bob Hope in a dress than the Hope Diamond, but she only said, "They're pretty."

"Oh, Ovid, and guess what; Magdelena di Lorenzo stopped by and rang the bell today."

He was on the ottoman, taking off his shoes and socks and rubbing his feet. "She in town? You invite her, come tonight, eat?"

"She was hurrying back upstate."

"Bella," he said sternly, pausing with his eyes looking up under his bushy eyebrows. "You *invite her*? This holy night, you no turn her away?"

"Of course I invited her, Ovid, I'm not a monster. She came to tell us that Renata has had a stroke or something, and is gone to an invalid home. She seems to be failing and cannot speak. Magdelena wanted to say thank you for the money you send every two weeks, and I think she is saying you ought not send it anymore, at least unless Renata recovers and comes home. She is a proud proud woman of the old country, that Magdelena. She doesn't want your help."

"Renata is our daughter-in-law still, even if she leave us behind."

"Why do you support her?" asked Laura. They had forgotten she was there.

"What a question, I ask you," said Nonno. "Help out, that what people do, Laura. Why you hang around with Mr. Sam downstairs, you having romance feelings?"

"Nonno!" Laura and Isabella Ciardi spoke the same word at once.

"Nice fellow," said Nonno, "but is too dark for you."

"The idea, Nonno," said Nonna. "Aren't we getting beyond that? When we come to this country in 1929, people called *us* too dark. We become Americans, we get on. For shame."

"No shame," said Nonno, "just reality. It hard to be unmatching. When you want marry, Laurita, I find you nice Italian boy."

"When we came into this country," Nonna said to Laura, "your grandfather considered changing our name from *Ciardi* to *Chase,* to sound more American."

"Why didn't you?" asked Laura.

"Because he couldn't pronounce *Chase* in a single syllable. It was *Chase*-ah."

"Back then, no could you, tootsie," said Nonno.

"We've come far, and we're still moving," agreed Nonna. Just then, dusk having fallen when no one was looking, the doorbell rang. Laura ran upstairs to get changed while Nonna steadied her hair and waited for Mary Bernice to answer the door and welcome in the first of the guests.

Laura tore through her clothes closet in the hallway. The blue corduroy jumper with two rhinestone pins at the yoke, the piqué shirt whose lace collar fell down like a collapsing doily around her neck. She dressed in the hall, afraid to peek into her room and see what business Hans might be up to next. Only a few hours now, if all went well.

She dared to open the door a crack before she went back downstairs, and was sorry that she had. Hans was crouching at the open window again. He had taken something—her nail file, perhaps?—and scratched lines in his right shoulder. She knew what that was for. Trying to find a wing rolled flag-like within, like a butterfly coiled up in a chrysalis.

Hans heard her at the door and jumped down, more graceful than Garibaldi. Though he put his arm out and his face was so stricken, Laura pulled back and avoided his embrace. "I have to get through this," she whispered. "No blood on my clothes, Hans. Hold on just a while longer. Please."

"Hungry," he said, and raised his wing in a backward, slicing motion, almost as a warrior might raise a spear. "Make me finished." Then he brought the wing down. At the top of the arc it was close to a beating, but the wing slowed as it fell, and it only touched Laura with the softest of pressure. She came within its partial shell. She could feel his heart beating in his bare chest and the blood pulsing in the fallen feathered canopy.

"They'd never believe a word of this in Miss Parsley's class," she found herself saying. "Good thing I'm not going back, because I'd be in detention for lying after the first sentence. What I did over my Christmas vacation."

"Hungry," he said again, and pressed her closer to him with his wing, as if he might ravish her and then eat her before somehow escaping into some other tell.

But she was strong, she pulled away, she said, "Later, you have to wait. But not for too long," and before he could stop her, she scooped up the nail file she saw on the top of her dresser. "Tonight, tonight." She grabbed her dancer's flats and fled down the stairs, tossing the nail file into an arrangement of evergreens and red Christmas tree ornaments that Nonna had artfully planted on the demi-lune outside the parlor door. Nonna was waiting in the shadows at the top of the main flight. She was choosing her moment to descend, so she waved Laura on.

By accident of timing they arrived at the same time, the fat Polumbos and the famous Zia Geneva and Mr. Corm Kennedy. They were squeezing through the vestibule and into the front hall with a false, kinetic cheer they couldn't possibly feel so early in the evening. Snow and slop everywhere. Hats and scarves unwrapping and falling away. Mary Bernice was on one side, taking coats. Nonno on the other, pumping Mr. Corm Kennedy's big pink hammy hand as if it were a wrench. The earlier gift of the poinsettia, in its paper sleeve and ribbons, had been forgotten in the front hall. Its presence lent an air of saucy informality and even something impromptu. Though of course perhaps Nonna had planned that, too. "It's from Signore Vincequerra," said Mary Bernice, squinting at the card. "He's had a dental emergency, poor dear, and will not be joining the Ciardi party this evening."

"So there *would* have been room for Nonna di Lorenzo," said Nonno to Laura, with an overeager, stagey smile.

"There is room for everyone," intoned Isabella

Ciardi, making her way down the stairs. Oh, even with the big mistake of the fake hair, she looked glamorous, she could be Dean Martin's mother or someone. She stopped halfway down the stairs and made a quarter-turn, as if to show off her legs and her outfit. She sported a skirt and a matching waist-length jacket in electric oranges and greens. The whole shebang was layered with clear beads, so she looked like a heap of garden vegetables after an ice storm. A heap of luxury vegetables, probably from Ciardi's Fine Foods and Delicacies. "Geneva, *è passato troppo tempo, perché mi fai soffrire?*"

"*Cara!*" cried the woman who wasn't the fat Mrs. Polumbo. Indeed, Zia Geneva was a paper clip twisted open to fullest extension. Weighed down by a huge pink leather pocketbook, she fell upon her sister's neck with cries of delight, as if she had swum all the way from Salerno to Staten Island and then caught the ferry and the uptown bus to get here in time.

The Polumbos smiled and handed over a box of ribbon candy and a bottle of Asti Spumante. Mrs. Polumbo looked like a lunch lady, and Mr. Polumbo a janitor, which turned out to be pretty close to the truth, except they worked for a parish rectory downtown, not a school.

Laura had hung back as far as she could, but she

had to submit to an ear-piercing hello and a crushing hug from Zia Geneva, who was strong for such a skinny bug. Then Laura was presented to Mr. Corm Kennedy. He had been looming behind everyone else, probably because as a newcomer his level of zest wasn't noisy enough, and anyway he wasn't Italian.

"Hey there, dollie," he said to Laura, and made a clicking sound in the back of his mouth and wrinkled up the side of his mouth, an aural version of a wink. Laura hated him at once. Still, she tried to keep her first wave of revulsion in check. He was stuck with the most famous name in the world right now, and he had none of the Kennedy attributes. He was taller than anyone else in the front hall, so what. And he was almost entirely without any hair—Nonna's wig would look better on him than on her. He had little half-glasses like Benjamin Franklin or someone, but he could never have played football at that famous compound in Hyannisport. Laura bet he had never run for a city bus. His middle was squishy, and his tobacco-colored vest could hardly button across his stomach. If he really had a lot of money it must be a sort of consolation prize by God. This was Zia Geneva's great late-life catch? Laura couldn't see it. Available cash must be a huge part of the attraction.

"We'll have a glass of something cheery in the

parlor, shall we, while Mary Bernice lays the table?" suggested Nonna. "Ovid, would you show the guests upstairs?"

"Isabella, what a gorgeous place on such a tight little tuck-away street. Did you do it all up yourself? I smell a lick of fresh paint—I hope not for us. We don't stand on ceremony, do we, Corm?"

"Not unless the ceremony involves a splash of bourbon," said Mr. Corm Kennedy. Laura caught the Polumbos giving each other a look.

"How'd you find a brownstone street here? Most of this neighborhood is brick," said Zia Geneva. "Lucky you. It looks so Brooklyn."

"Maybe wrong materials get delivered wrong address," said Nonno. "Driver he probably m—"

Nonna coughed to keep him from saying *mick*.

"Mobster," said Nonno. "Mobster from Palermo."

"It's a beaut," said Mr. Corm Kennedy. "Three floors?"

"Basement plus four," said Nonno. "Last owner put illegal top floor, step back from street. Not us. We keep laws right and good."

"Do you need help bringing up the food?" Laura asked Mary Bernice.

"Most of it is plated and sitting in a nice oven," replied the cook. "And I've got those fancy domes your grandfather borrowed from the store, the ones that keep food warm on the table. You go up there with your folks, now, and make pretty, like a good girl."

"I haven't qualified for 'good girl' since I was seven," said Laura, but Mary Bernice waved her off.

"Mary Bernice," called Nonna over her shoulder, "if it is all laid out and you have nothing better to do, why don't you run the extra poinsettia around the block to old Mrs. Steenhauser? She's a widow neighbor, lives behind us," she explained to the guests, "and we try to look in from time to time." She simpered like the Spirit of Extra Niceness.

"Of course I have nothing better to do," muttered Mary Bernice, but this was a good time for her to take her comments back to the kitchen and deliver them to Garibaldi, so she did.

"We'll want to see the *whole* house," Zia Geneva was gushing at the top of the first flight. "Is that your office in there? You've done so well, Ovid. Business must be booming to support a fancy home like this. Nothing like Hester Street. Not even Bensonhurst, where I was with dear Paolo. But you don't mind all the Germans? It's Germantown around here," she added to Mr. Corm Kennedy.

"Parlor beyond, front of house, come, come," said Nonno theatrically. They moved into the parlor.

"Isn't it grand," said Mr. Corm Kennedy, rather flatly, waiting for his drink.

"We got it for song," said Nonno, "auction by city for tax cheat or something."

Nonna frowned at her husband over her sister's shoulder; that wasn't the script they were supposed to be following. She touched her sister's elbow. "You are downright chic, Geneva, love suits you; you are so elegant!"

"*Peww peww, stai scherzando, sembro una merda.*"

"Hey, no secret sister talk, you promised," said her beau, loomingly.

"And what you do, sir?" Mr. Polumbo said to Mr. Corm Kennedy. Everyone paused because this was probably rude to ask out loud. Kennedys didn't do things, they just *had* things.

But Mr. Corm Kennedy didn't seem to mind the question. He threw back a healthy swallow of whatever Nonno had given him and he said, "Mostly I just make money. Investments out in the Texas area."

"Oil?" asked Mrs. Polumbo, the first thing she'd said so far.

"In a manner of speaking. Corn oil. How'd you find this place, Ovid?" asked Mr. Corm Kennedy, taking in the flocked wallpaper. The crucifix. The fringed lamp-shades. The nineteenth-century stamped tin Roman medallions, probably notices of special intentions for prayer, hung on the wall above the Zenith television packed into its console. The famous reproduction of David doing his sex-maniac thing on the corner table. The oil painting of Nonno, Nonna, and their teenage son Giuseppe hanging over the mantel, looking like a commercial advertisement for an old-world family-style tomato sauce recipe.

"That hair," Geneva was saying to Isabella. "You've always been so brave, Bella. I wouldn't have the strength of heart to walk into Grand Central Station looking so Mussolini about it. How I admire you."

"Jenny," said Nonna, "I do it for you, to make you feel better about yourself." But this wasn't mean, this was sisters joking, and they were both downing their sparkling whatever. Doughty Mrs. Polumbo held her drink, untasted, in her hands and tried not to stare straight at David's signal attribute, which was at her precise eye level three feet away and seemed to be the only thing paying attention to her.

"But she's beautiful, too," Zia Geneva was saying, about Laura. "A credit to us Bentivengos. Mama and Papa, *come sarebbero venuti se potessero vederla!* Stunning. A comfort to you in your old age, you nonna!"

"Not that old, Jenny," said Nonna.

"Older than me. I don't suppose she's smart? But

doesn't matter, never matter, with beauty like that. Such happiness, you deserve it all, Bella, after such sorrow, my darling. At least you got your Ovid still, after all these years, and what do you think of my very own Kennedy, Bella? Tell me true while they're deep in tales of the stock exchange."

"He looks like a standing lamp," said Nonna. "Very tall."

"Tall enough for what matters, Bella."

"*Basta,* Jenny."

"I mean enough to change the lightbulb in the pantry!"

"Mr. Corm Kennedy," said Nonno, "you come by Ciardi's while you in city, I fix you up good with Parma ham and best imported pesto you ever meet."

"Already been by," said the guest. His hosts looked stunned. Uh-oh, thought Laura. "I dropped by today to introduce myself and have a look around."

"Nobody introduce nobody to me?" said Nonno with a strained smile.

"Thought I'd pick up a house gift for you as a kind of joke," said Mr. Corm Kennedy, "but I couldn't find anything I thought you'd like. Awfully busy store today, though. Didn't want to interrupt anyone at the cash registers. Ca-*ching.*" He winked at Laura. "Ca-*ching* is Italian for *moola.*"

"We brought something else," said Geneva. "I almost forgot. Where's my purse?" She had dropped the huge thing by the side of the sofa, and now she scrabbled at the clasp and withdrew a flat parcel wrapped in red and green paper. Great, thought Laura. Another *Peter, Paul and Mary.* But it wasn't.

It was two phonograph albums wrapped in the same paper. One was a recording of Rossini's *La Cenerentola,* which Laura guessed Nonno might already have. "Goodness Triumphant" it said under the title as the album was passed around so everyone could admire it. "Jenny tells me you like the old-fogey stuff," said Mr. Corm Kennedy, "so this seemed as good as any of them. You know it?"

"I heard of it," said Nonno stiffly.

"Then for balance, this other one. Less stodgy, you know?"

It was called *The Electrifying Aretha Franklin.* "Now that baby doll can sing," said Mr. Corm Kennedy. "Put this on at night to get comfy, if you know what I mean. 'You Made Me Love You.' Does the trick. Gotta hear it. You have a phonograph player?"

"Now?" said Nonno. "You mean now?"

"We have a portable hi-fi," said Nonna quickly. "It's upstairs. Laura, can you go get it? Remember to unplug it first and latch the lid. Don't let the cord drag or you might trip. And put *La Sonnambula* back in its paper sleeve? Can you manage?"

"I'm not an idiot," said Laura, glad for the chance to escape the nightmare of grown-up society.

She closed the parlor door after she passed through. Downstairs, she heard the front door slam. Mary Bernice heading out in the storm with the poor unwanted poinsettia. She was probably going to walk to the river and toss it overboard. The house was redolent of fish; it was a veritable harborside of smells. Mary Bernice must have finished setting up already but had been too annoyed to come upstairs to announce it yet. She was cooling off with an outdoor chore. Laura knew how she felt.

The record player in her grandparents' bedroom wasn't too heavy to carry, but Laura watched her step coming back downstairs anyway. The noise in the parlor was picking up. Maybe the prickliness was wearing off. "Here you go," said Laura.

Mr. Corm Kennedy took it upon himself to set up Nonno's precious hi-fi on the table with the statue of David, whose gaze now appeared to be trying to read the record label as it spun. A sultry, glazed accompaniment of strings and some relaxed woodwind or saxophone turned the Ciardi parlor into a kind of cocktail lounge. Mrs. Polumbo visibly stiffened and Mr. Polumbo patted her hand. "Voodoo music," said Mrs. Polumbo, sotto voce.

"I didn't want to do it, I didn't want to do it," sang Miss Aretha Franklin.

"Another drink," said Nonno, getting into the spirit of things.

"Now you're talking," said Mr. Corm Kennedy, and then to Laura, "Crank that thing up, will you, kitten?"

"I can't think how you afford such a home," said Zia Geneva. "Will you show me everything, Bella? Corm has the pokiest little penthouse on Louisburg Square, not enough room to skin a cat. Is that the phrase? Though there's the Vineyard of course."

"Mr. Corm Kennedy have vineyard?" asked Nonno. "Sangiovese grape perhaps, like Chianti?"

Something ticked, some noise from downstairs got through the commotion of the popular music. "Would you go downstairs and see how Mary Bernice is getting on?" asked Nonna softly to Laura. "We don't want to drink too much on an empty stomach, and the Ritz crackers and cream cheese are vanishing." Too soon for Mary Bernice to be back, thought Laura, unless she just junked the plant in the gutter somewhere.

Laura's stomach twisted in a different way, a frightened way. She left the parlor and closed the door. She half wished she had a key so she could lock them all in.

She was halfway down the stairs when she heard the clatter of food domes hitting the carpet, the breaking of china. She knew what she would see, she had always known it, somehow. The sliding dining room doors, stuck in their open position, had nothing to hide. Hans was squatting on the table, his swung wing knocking over wineglasses and flowers, his hand rushing fistful after fistful of eels, brandade, lobster tail, the rest of it to his mouth. He drank a third of the tureen of bisque and threw the tureen to the floor when he couldn't get to the liquid pooled behind the broad lip. "Stop," said Laura, "stop, stop," but it was already too late, much too late. Much too late for anything.

She grabbed the carving knife from its usual place on the sideboard. Hans paused, sickened, dazed with animal surfeit, and turned his left shoulder and extended his wing, a gesture that said, Slice it off, slice here.

"Get upstairs before I kill you," she said.

His expression was inscrutable, but then it had always been so, hadn't it? She advanced, and he made an inhuman sound, low in his throat, but it was only the sort of grief that can never fully dislodge itself from the human breast—from any breast, maybe. He disappeared up the back stairs.

27

Nonna was leading the party down the front staircase. "Careful there, Cormac," sang out Zia Geneva. "You'll take a tumble, you'll spend Christmas Eve in Mount Sinai."

"It all smells swell," said Mr. Corm Kennedy. "Been looking forward to this."

"A tradition we cherish," said Nonno, though the Ciardis had only occasionally worked themselves up to a whole feast of the seven fishes—they usually got through about four recipes and were too exhausted to keep going.

Nonna turned at the bottom step and saw Laura in the door of the dining room. Beyond, Nonna caught a glimpse of the mayhem, the snapshot edge of spatter and fracture, and she turned on her heel and clapped her hands. “Change of plans,” she said briskly. “Panetta’s.”

“Bella?” asked Nonno.

“Panetta’s,” she said. “They’ll be able to squeeze six of us in. *Non discutere con me ora, Vito. Dopo. Andiamo.*”

“There seven of us,” said Nonno, circling his finger.

“Laura is under the weather, she’s staying home,” said Nonna. With her arms folded across her lacquered bosom, she stood like a crossing guard in the middle of the hall, forcing the guests to their coats and hats on the rack by the front door.

“But it smells like *heaven*,” said Zia Geneva in a whine. “You tease us, Bella!”

“One of the fish turns out to be bad. You never know with fish. Nonno, hurry ahead and get a table.”

“At such hour on *Christmas Eve*?” Nonno couldn’t move his thinking as fast as his wife.

“You’ll get the table,” replied Nonna. “Please. *You’re Signore Ovid Ciardi.* That means something in this city.”

He shrugged himself into his coat and plopped his fedora on his head and scurried out. “Snow on snow, watch your stepfoots,” he called behind him.

“What the devil?” asked Mary Bernice, coming

back from her chore. She was hiking up the stoop to the front door instead of using the kitchen entrance, for once, so she could interrogate the departing guests. "Don't tell me. Not enough salt in the béarnaise?"

"See to it, Mary Bernice," said Nonna. "All of it. Laura will help."

"Well, I do love a sudden change of plans, makes me feel young," Zia Geneva was trilling, sounding like some old bat escaped from a nursing home. Mary Bernice shut the front door behind them.

"For the love of Christ, are you going to tell me what the hell is going on?" she asked Laura. They retreated down the hall to the dining room. Laura swept a hand out, as if saying, Here's my science project. Mary Bernice shrieked. Laura gave her a sideways hug, fierce though somewhat false. "What happened?" asked Mary Bernice, sobbing.

"Garibaldi?" said Laura, tentatively.

"But I locked him in my room! Where is he now?"

"He must have got out. I just put him back there."

The damage wasn't as bad as it had first looked. Two broken soup bowls and one plate, and three cracked wineglasses. Most of the food was spilled on the tablecloth, so when they rolled up the white linen and bundled it away, the wreckage was manageable. Mary Bernice kept blowing her nose and wiping her eyes on the napkins Laura had ironed. "They'll come back for dessert," said Mary Bernice. "Get the Hoover."

Before she turned on the appliance, though, Mary Bernice pivoted to face Laura closely. "No cat ever did this much damage unless it was a cougar," she said. "Something else is in this house, Laura. And I don't like it one bit. It's been keeping out of sight but not very well, and you'd best do something about it before your grandparents have a double-action stroke. My grandmother had the evil eye and I didn't inherit more than an evil blink, but every now and then it comes over me. Listen to me: Something isn't right here."

"I don't have any idea what you're talking about," said Laura, and in a certain way she was telling the truth. She still didn't have any idea what was going on, or why. But she agreed that it had to stop.

You weren't supposed to be afraid of a miracle, were you? Maybe the young virgin Mary had been terrified. Maybe she hadn't wanted the job. Whoever could know how to handle such mystery. But Laura was afraid to go upstairs.

She sat on the bottom step, waiting for her grandparents to come home. The maître d' must have found a table for Signore Ciardi. Of course he had. Laura hoped the lights were turned down *very* low. Panetta's was no place to take guests in order to impress them. It was standard fare for a certain nondiscriminating clientele, with red-checkered tablecloths pocked with holes in the fabric, and candles stuck in bulbous green glass bottles wrapped in rattan. Every dish arrived with the same red sauce, probably even the ice cream. According to Nonna, it must come out of a spigot direct from Little Italy.

Mary Bernice tramped through with her coat on. "I'm going home to Ted," she said to Laura. "If you're up when your grandparents come in, tell them I'm fed up. I've had it. To work a whole week and have my work sabotaged? Bloody hell. I'll be in on Boxing Day. If I still have a job. I'll get blamed for this somehow—the help always does. Merry Christmas."

Out of her coat pocket she withdrew a small plastic vial in the shape of the Virgin. The crown of stars was a plastic screw-top, which she removed. She sprinkled some water into the dining room and made the sign of the Cross. She then walked to the waiting room and opened the door, and sprinkled the false wing lying dead in its shadows. Then the Christmas tree. For good measure she jerked her hand up the stairwell and water hung in the air before beading onto the polished stairs. "Holy water from Lourdes," said the cook, "and may it do a little good. My sister brought it for me a few years ago and I've been saving it for an emergency. There's enough left for Ted's heart attack if he ever has one. So long, Laura, and may the peace of Christ descend upon this house and beat a little sense into you."

Laura crept upstairs on her knees as if on a pilgrimage. In the parlor she took Aretha Franklin off the turntable and put on *La Cenerentola,* at a lower volume. "A story of Cinderella," said the record sleeve. In Italian, big surprise. She let side one play to the end, and when she heard the front door opening, she set the needle down in the first track again, and hustled herself farther upstairs.

She couldn't go into her room, though. She was frightened of what she might do, and what she might not do, and what Hans might do, and what he might not do. She crouched at the top of her stairs, holding on to the newel post. The diners returned. It seemed as if they were taking their desserts in the dining room after all, and mounting the stairs to the parlor for a last round of drinks. Even Mrs. Polumbo sounded as if she had warmed up some. She probably adored Panetta's.

Laura stayed there, hunched in the dark, for what felt like several nights, while the guests lingered and loitered. Nonno must have gone up to their bedroom to get *Peter, Paul and Mary* without Laura hearing him, because "500 Miles" began to ghost up the stairwell like a prophecy.

At last the guests left, fluting farewells and *buon*

Natale. Nonno's and Nonna's footsteps as they made their way upstairs after the final goodbyes were much slower than they'd been all evening. They were talking to each other in low voices as if they expected Laura to be asleep. But before the bedroom door closed, one of them stumped to the bottom of the attic steps—and then started up. So it wasn't Nonna, she couldn't manage that. Laura sprang up and showed herself at the top of the steps before he got very far.

"You awake," Nonno said. "I think so. I tell Nonna you still awake. Laurita, we talk about this tomorrow, Christmas Day or no Christmas Day. You tell us why you leave Miss Aretha Franklin and come downstairs and make trash and war in our house. When so much depend on good time for guests. You tell us why you ruin us."

"I—" she began.

"You tell us tomorrow," he reminded her. "Tomorrow. Now, you just tell me one thing, and I go sleep and count my blessings anyway and curse my fate. Laura. You tell me. You good? You good, Laura?"

She said, "I can't tell."

His face fell and he began to haul himself up to the next step to look at her expression more closely. "I can't tell," she said again, "but I'll tell you tomorrow. Go to sleep, Nonno. Tell Nonna I'm sorry."

"*You* tell Nonna. Tomorrow," he said. "Now, I tell her you asleep. She rest better if she think so. Even if a lie. You lose your mind like your mother, or you just a silly girl, who know, nobody but *Gesù* know. But Nonna need to sleep. So do you. Go to sleep."

28

Nonno didn't put on an aria tonight. It was too late and the record player was still downstairs in the parlor. Laura waited at the top of the stairs, still as ice. She heard Nonno begin to snore almost at once, and then she heard Nonna crying a little and blowing her nose. Nonna sounded like a kitten issuing little asthmatic snorts all on the same note. They didn't last for long. The water rang in the master bathroom sink, the toilet flushed, the house grew quiet.

A house knows when almost everyone else is asleep. It either grows more relaxed or more alert at that moment, depending.

Laura wasn't certain which way the mood was tending tonight, but the time had come, for good or for ill. Her grandparents were asleep. Hans could stay no longer.

She found him in her room, squatting on her bed, the knees of her brother's jeans nearly touching his outthrust chin. Somehow Hans had located another shirt of her brother's, a long-sleeved Oxford one, and he had managed to get his arm in the sleeve and more or less pull the other side about him like a shawl, skipping the wing and joining at the waist. Laura straightened his collar, buttoned his cuff, and did up the bottom two buttons of the shirt. It wouldn't afford much warmth, but Laura wasn't sure how much Hans felt the cold. And even if he did, it wasn't the most urgent problem they had.

"We are going now," she said. "We are following the baby owl."

"We?"

"I will bring you as far as I can go."

He went to the window and looked out into the snow. It was about midnight on Christmas Eve and a few church bells were ringing in the old-fashioned way of parishes back home across the ocean. "Not the window, not that way," said Laura. "You have to stay somewhat human a little while longer. We'll do the stairs, now I know you can manage them."

She turned off the light in her disheveled room. He

looked about himself in the dark, as if only seeing the room for the first time as he saw it for the last, and then he lunged forward and touched his mouth to hers. A wild, unnatural energy, full of threat and portent and angelic magnificence. One hand gripping the doorknob to her room, her other hand lacing into the curls at his right temple, she didn't pull away. His wing stuttered upward like a Venetian blind with a broken cord on one side, rising on its other side in a fanning vector of pleats and shadows.

They made their way down the attic steps, past the doors to the master bedroom and Nonna's sewing room; down the next flight past the doors to the parlor and Nonno's office; downstairs past the open broken doors to the dining room. In the waiting room, Laura picked up the artificial wing. "Let me carry it," she said to Hans, "for a while. This is as close to being a swan as I am going to get."

Garibaldi came skulking out of the shadows of the dining room. He didn't yowl or hiss at Hans, but came and sat neatly near the doormat by the front door, as if ready to accept his station again as king animal in this house of human woe. He looked up at Hans with as much respect as a cat ever can seem to show—not much—and then yawned and looked away.

Laura found her coat and gloves and she put on her

grandfather's fedora. She pulled on her black rubber boots. There were no boots for Hans, but he'd arrived with bare feet—so there was nothing else for it. Then she pressed the button in the front door so it wouldn't lock behind her.

The snow was still falling. Van Pruyn Place was empty. The last footprints had already begun to fill in, and the parked cars had become soft humps. The black iron palings in the front yards were swollen with white icing.

Laura carried the wing under her arm as she imagined an art student might carry a big portfolio. His wing on his left side, hers on the right, they touched wingless shoulders as they trod down the middle of the street toward East End Avenue.

No moment of enchantment ever empties Manhattan of its night owls, and here and there in the distance as they crossed the avenue Laura could make out the red taillights of disappearing traffic. Churchgoers late for midnight Mass, and partygoers and skulkers and loners, they all showed as human silhouettes, dark against the white snow, never very close. They came and went as Laura and Hans came and went, uptown a little, crosstown the next block, along the decorated median strip of Park Avenue, crosstown again. Laura leading the way, trying to make the walk last, taking long ways around. Detours to delay finality. The great bluff-faces of Park Avenue apartments were lost in the uplift of snow. Snow gyring from black nothingness into the faces of Hans and Laura, settling along the fledges of their wings.

They reached Central Park and entered it north of the museum. They rounded the palace of art and ventured deeper into the park. The world became more disoriented. Snow turned Laura around. She clung to Hans, she laced her arm through his, she took off the glove of her left hand so her cold fingers could feel the warmth underneath her brother's shirtsleeve for the last time. Then their hands linked. Chained, they pushed on, stumbled on, across paths and beneath trees.

They came upon that odd cluster of statuary, Alice in Wonderland and her creatures, covered in white and looking ready to stop holding their breath and to break out of their ice casing. They skirted a formal reflecting pool with beveled edges. A little farther on, Hans Christian Andersen himself. The ugly duckling at his shin was up to his breast feathers in drift.

She knew where they were now, roughly, but she couldn't let him go yet. They stumbled and held themselves together until she could delay it no longer. The Plaza was beginning to loom ahead, and the city would start up again there. They couldn't go back to the city.

They turned. The world regularized itself into huge and natural symmetry. They were alone in the grand concourse of elms, walking north with their wings. Not just alone together, the way couples are in New York, but alone in the world. Snow on Christmas Eve, or early on Christmas morning now, had cloaked the population of the entire world, and removed it. Only the hundreds of lit windows from buildings on the East Side and the West Side apartment mansions proved that Hans and Laura had not fully left the world of time and human agency.

At the top of Bethesda Terrace they paused. They were higher than that noble statue perched in the emptied and snowy concrete pond below. They could see its flared wings like the hood ornament of a fancy automobile. It was promise of some sort, or so it seemed to Laura.

In any event, it was the only rescue idea she had ever had.

Down the unshoveled and sloppy steps they made their way, slipping and clutching each other for balance. There were hardly any other words to say, except when they reached the edge of the pond basin, Laura managed to get Hans's attention by squeezing his hand tightly. He turned his face to hers.

"Do you know where you are going?" she asked him.

"Away from here," he said. "That's all I know."

She wanted to ask him if he would look for his baby sister, his human brothers, but then she thought: No, he has flown away from them once because he could not bear to be other than wholly human. Now he has to try the alternative. He really doesn't have a choice. Do we.

She bade him to raise his arm outstretched and level. Using the strips from her ripped bedsheet, she tied on the crazy armature of wing the way she had tied it onto Sam Roscoe. In the snowlight, the goose-down feathers seemed to have multiplied, or maybe that was snow upon them, thickening them up. For a rush job, it was a nearly convincing item, that wing.

He didn't touch her again, he didn't look at her again, he didn't speak to her again, he didn't clasp her in his wings, he didn't pause as he leaped in his bare feet upon the ridge of Bethesda Fountain. All she said was "Godspeed," because she could think of nothing else. He probably didn't hear her anyway. The wind had picked up, the snow was clotting into paste, gumming her eyes and wiping out most of what she could see. He may have made it into the air as a swan-boy, but by the time he alighted on the left shoulder of the Bethesda angel, he was less boy, less real. His prison, his release. He was probably a swan. Anyway, there was a shape like a swan in the storm.

It was Christmas Day now, but he didn't sing a carol to her. Later, she was glad of this, when she remembered that a swan only sings as he is about to die. He left her without a word, and without a song.

29

A week later, Laura boarded the Delaware and Hudson train that ran from Grand Central Station to Montreal. She had a small suitcase stored at her feet—a Christmas present from Nonno and Nonna. She had a sack of hazelnut chocolates and wrapped Amaretto biscuits and a few bars of lavender soap in fancy paper. She sat on the left-hand side of the train, watching the Hudson River pulse northward with its tidal appetite, past cliffs and mountains that had reminded early settlers of the Rhineland. The sky was a peerless, top-of-the-morning blue, straight out of County Tyrone and no mistake, Mary Bernice had told her.

Laura had never taken a train by herself before—indeed she'd never been in the New York City subway system without a friend or relative—so this trip was a challenge and a proposition. She had to manage this alone, said Nonno. She had to prove she was ready to take on some responsibility, for he and Nonna were getting too old to keep tending her as if she were a child.

The hills were black and icy, the little trackside towns like toy sets. People who lived outside of New York City were too friendly. Laura had to fend off nosy conversations in order to be able to think about what had happened. And how it had come about. And what was next. She opened a hardcover copy of *Franny and Zooey* and let it rest on her lap, showing pages of smart dense type. Her eye often fell upon it as if she were ruminating over its mysteries thoughtfully. Once in a while she remembered to turn a page. But she was only reading her own thoughts, really.

He'd been gone a week, had Hans, and the world had settled into a normalcy that only partly resembled what had gone before.

Christmas Day or not, Nonna had lit into Laura like, as Mary Bernice put it, an Italian banshee. "Don't give me that crap," she said to her granddaughter, using an expression Laura had never heard the Italian matriarch utter before. "No cat turns a whole table upside down no matter how much he likes fish. There wasn't time. He hasn't the strength. You did this. You are a bitter, angry, broken child, and who can blame you for any of that, but you are still responsible for your behavior, young lady. How close you came to ruining us, you'll never know, for I'll never tell you."

"Tell me, why don't you," said Laura. "Go ahead. I dare you. What's left to lose?"

"All right, I'll tell you then. Miss Uppity-in-Charge. Tell you all the risks we've taken to better ourselves for thirty-five years. Tell you again about the loss of a son who might have helped us with the work at this stage of our old lives. Tell you, all right since you asked, about all the cash we've sent to help Nonna di Lorenzo with our daughter-in-law, your poor blighted mama. Not to mention your school fees, did I mention that? I won't mention it. Nonno builds Ciardi's Fine Foods and Delicacies up from a single packing crate on the Lower East Side to this establishment known up and down the eastern seaboard for the best in continental, what's the word, confections and comestibles, all the imported stuff rich people like to eat to make them feel rich. And to make them feel less alone in godless New York. All these years, we crawl out of the gutters of Rome and the slums of Salerno and the dumps of Hester Street and we somehow survive the Depression and the War and we lose first our son and then our grandson, life is no fair, and we are left with only you to console us. And you're too young to help yet. Then Nonno overextends with this house, and takes out a second mortgage, and that fool shop Buccelli's with its cut-rate junk opens over on Second Avenue, and suddenly we are losing our footing. Losing our shirt, losing our way, losing our minds, do I have to spell it out?"

"I get it," said Laura. "Stop screaming. Don't get excited, Nonna. Cardiac alert."

"And our one hope is that Mr. Richie Rich Corm Kennedy, maybe he wants to invest in a shop that is a real going concern, because he falls in love with crazy Jenny, who frankly is the one who should be in a lockup facility, but who am I to say, I love her but she is nuts."

"Take a sip of water, Nonna."

"And here he comes all the way from Boston, Massachusetts, and we put on the dog for him, is that the saying? We put on the dog. I work my fingers to the bone and not to mention poor Mary Bernice, I can't say about her now, it makes me crazy. And then you leave us all in the parlor listening to that sexpot Miss Aretha Franklin, I don't know about her, maybe her voice makes *you* a little nuts like your Zia Geneva. You waltz downstairs and you bash up the work of a week and you risk the work of a lifetime."

Laura had nothing she could say to this. She studied her hands in her lap. Garibaldi was inching around the parlor as if smelling for traces of Hans.

"And should it all come tumbling down? Should we take a bunkbed in the poorhouse and piss in a clay pot like we did in the old country? And you know why I am not killing you right this minute, I am so angry?"

"Nonna, please, she just girl," said Nonno, with one hand over both his eyes. "She no need to hear all this."

"Because Mr. Corm Kennedy, he *like* Panetta's!" shouted Nonna. She was sounding more and more like her husband. "All that cooking we do, and he think crummy Panetta's is real Italy! It make him feel rich and superior to us, better than us instead of family with the same degree of rich. I could spit. He swan out of there with his big fat bald-headed smile and he pat Nonno on his shoulder like he some pushcart sandwich king or somebody—"

"*Isabella,*" said Nonno sternly. "I got dignity, some left. Leave alone."

"He agree to come in as partner," spat Nonna. She breathed out little gusts like a lapdog and spoke more quietly then. "The whole thing is good, is rotten, it works, not because we are equals, but because he thinks he is rescuing us."

"Who care what he think?" said Nonno. "Cash is cash."

"He thinks he can buy his way into our family!" said Nonna.

"Isn't that what you wanted?" asked Laura.

"Yes, yes, you idiot child. So we not ruined on Christmas morning, thank you *Gesù* and Mary and the angel on the stable. But no thanks to you, Laura. You act so proper but you go and try and ruin us. And all because we have to send you to Montreal."

"So much anger," Nonno said sadly. "You have to be addled now, Laura, and kill anger inside you. It bad, you kill it or it kill you."

"Yes, Nonno," said Laura, sensing that *l'agitazione* was dying down.

The first time the girl had thought in Italian, as far as she could remember. Yes? Maybe.

"Why you so angry?" he asked her. "You no have father, you no have mother, your brother he die. But you have us who love you so much, too much. We not enough for you? No, we not enough for you! But we not nothing."

"You're not nothing," Laura agreed. "But if all you have left is me, how can you send me to Montreal?"

"They won't let you back in that school," said Nonna. She downed a tablet of something. "We've been over this, Laura. We don't want you in public school where bad things happen to girls like you. And the Catholic schools, they require better grades than the grades you get. Driscoll School was working just about good enough, and then you ruin it, the way you ruin our dinner party last night. Montreal is the only place we know of. It comes recommended by Monsignor."

"I've told you a hundred times, it was an accident," said Laura. "I didn't mean to break Maxine Sugargarten's nose. Anyway she's getting a nose job out of it, so she is kind of grateful."

"The headmaster, he tells me that they worry you have no friends, that you don't know how to make friends. You are, what is the word, isolated and disapproving. Superior."

"If no one likes me because I'm so stupid, how can I be superior? How can I like them?" asked Laura, and her eyes, her stupid eyes, filled with stupid tears.

"So this Maxine liking you now because you break her nose?" asked Nonno.

"Yeah well, she likes the idea of her new nose."

Nonna said, "You break my *heart,* Laura, you really do. Tell you what. Christmas mercy from mean old Nonna. You get one more chance—you write to Mr. G. at Driscoll School and you tell him you have learned your lesson and you want another chance. You realize all this anger, it is too much. You do realize this? It can't hurt, though I doubt it can help. Mr. G. thinks that Driscoll is not a good place for you. But I will mail a letter from you, and if he changes his mind, we will agree to reconsider Montreal. Ovid, you good with this?"

"I am in," he said. "Hope is strong but you have to work for hope. Now we get up please on our feet, and go to Mass and pray for a Christmas miracle, and you write a good letter and Mr. G. say yes. We already miss the ten A.M."

"We missed the High Mass?" shrieked Nonna. "Curses upon the Ciardi house. Mrs. Pill is in the country and I was supposed to do the coffees."

"Maybe some Christmas miracle happen, somebody else make coffee," said Nonno.

"*Dammi la forza.* Oh well, hurry up. If we make the eleven we'll pick up some bagels on the way home. Did I say, Zia Geneva and Mr. Corm Kennedy are coming back for dinner tonight."

Nonno said firmly, "Pasta puttanesca. Anchovies, capers, little red wine. Nothing more fancy. In kitchen like family. Get what you pay for."

A couple of days later, Maxine Sugargarten and Donna Flotarde came over to Van Pruyn Place. Donna played with Garibaldi until he scratched her. "Ow. It's always injury and assault with you, isn't it, Laura," said Donna, and flounced away through the snow to go see Doll Pettigrew and her new beautifying kit in its mint-blue leatherette case.

Maxine and Laura worked all afternoon on a letter to Mr. G. Not easy. Laura tried to explain all over again that while it was true that she had borrowed the record album from Maxine's locker, it wasn't wrecked or ruined like everything else Laura touched, and she *had* given it back, after all. And the blood and emergency room was a distraction to the plain truth of it, which is that she and Maxine were now friends, like Shari Lewis and Lamb Chop, only one of them was not a puppet.

Maxine asked Laura to come over to her house. Laura met Maxine's big brother Spike, home from basic training. They all listened to Bobby Vee. Spike acted as if he found himself to be really cool but he wasn't, he was almost as boring as Maxine used to be.

A couple of days later Mr. Grackowicz rang the house. He kept Nonna on the line for a long time, but Laura couldn't hear what Nonna was saying, since the cagey old sinner kept her hand over her mouth and the mouthpiece, and she muttered. When she hung up, she told Laura that Mr. G. had to be in the neighborhood that evening for an emergency finance committee meeting about raising funds to repair the broken pipes. So Nonna had invited him to come by for a little refreshment. Then she rang up Nonno at the store and told him to bring a small ham, a bottle of Campari, and a tin of almond biscuits that weren't too stale.

The arrangement of bribes in the parlor—underneath the statue of ever-vigilant David—was, thought Laura, a pretty good sign that Mr. G. was weakening. Nonna made Laura put on a dress that made her look—thank you so much, Nonna, you and your sense of style can go back to Italy—like a teenage Shirley Temple foundering in a reform school for wayward girls. For herself, Nonna bravely tossed off the wig and showed up in her grey prison hairdo, in a powder-blue twinset with pearls and a huge cross on a chain dragging at her around the neck. She had done without rouge. Maybe she was trying for a look of leukemia. The sympathy strategy.

Nonno poured a stiff drink, but Mr. G. just wanted a cup of tea because, he said, it wouldn't do any good for him to walk into a finance committee meeting sporting the aroma of indulgence. Mary Bernice brought in the tea, and before she left she said, "I have an opinion, too, you know, though nobody ever asks me."

Nonno and Nonna were so startled at her talking out of turn that they were speechless. Mr. G. said, kindly enough, "Well, what would that be?"

"You want to keep her away from the nuns if you possibly can," said Mary Bernice. "They're good women, most of them, but they either convert you or they help you lose your faith too early, if you ask me. And I'm Irish, so I know whereof I speak."

"So I can tell," said Mr. G.

He talked to Nonno and Nonna, who nodded and sputtered only a little, but Laura couldn't get the gist of how the negotiation was going. Then, starting to sum things up, he said to the grandparents, "May I talk with Miss Ciardi by herself for a moment, please?"

"Of course, you our guest," said Nonno, heaving himself up out of his easy chair. "We go next door to office, we find little something for donate to burst pipes."

"No need for that, Mr. Ciardi." When they had gone, Mr. Grackowicz turned to Laura, who had been standing close to the mantelpiece with her hands clasped in front of her waist like a waitress at Frombacher's Viennese Café on East 86th and Madison. "Laura. I have a question to ask, and I don't want you to lie. Did you write this letter all by yourself?"

She tried to gather her thoughts and to assess what he wanted to hear, and he saw her confusion. "Wait," he said. "Let me put it another way. Someone else helped you write this letter. Am I right? Tell the truth."

Her face dropped. "How did you know?" she said in a small voice.

"Well, it wasn't either of your grandparents, I can tell that," he said, "and it wasn't you alone, Laura. I know your work. You have a reputation for refusing to hand in your writing assignments. You say you can't write. So who was it? Was it your cook? Or someone from school? A student?"

There was no point in lying now—Laura realized the jig was up, as they said in the movies. The gambit hadn't worked. "It was Maxine Sugargarten," she admitted. "We worked on it together. I'm sorry."

"I'm not," he replied. "Or not too much."

She couldn't figure him out. "What do you mean?"

He drained his teacup and looked around, as if wishing he had decided on something stronger after all. "School isn't only about learning to write and read, though it is mostly that. It's also about learning how to manage friendships. How to get along. You've always been very strong with the younger kids, but you've been isolated from children your own age. Your peers. A lot of your problems have come from holding yourself out from them, as if you're something special."

"Something special about covers it," she said, making a face.

"That's not what I mean. I'm saying that if you and Maxine, who is in your grade, have been able to patch up your differences so you could work together with her on this letter, this shows a new ability to collaborate. And a lot of learning, especially for girls like you, comes from friendship. I'm encouraged just enough by the fact of this campaign, and that it was conceived and carried out by the both of you, to let you have one more try. On probation till Easter. We'll reassess then, and see if you have been able to build on this beginning. But I'll be requiring some heavy lifting from you, Laura. You'll have to spread your wings now."

"Oh," said Laura. "Well, I have some practice there."

That night Laura had gone to her first sleepover ever. The Sugargartens' was a cramped, five-room railroad flat two stories above a mattress warehouse showroom on Third Avenue. "I like it here. It has a lot of character," said Laura.

"Tell me about character," said Maxine's mother, pouring herself another glass of rye whiskey and Fanta. "I never picked up the concept. Does having a goddamn nose job come into it?"

It wasn't going to be easy, this friendship thing, but Laura was determined to try to make it work. Maxine got annoyed that Laura had to get changed into her nightgown in the bathroom, such a prude! and went sulky for about fifteen minutes. But after lights-out, they flopped down on blankets spread on the floor of Maxine's tiny bedroom and whispered. It was the closest Laura had ever lain to someone except for the swan-brother. The subjects were: vacations, crummy teachers, the other girls, which boys you liked and which ones you liked best and which one you would kiss if you absolutely had to or someone in your family would *die*. Laura was so busy trying to keep up with the conversation that there wasn't a moment in which she could pause and try out her answers by telling herself into a story sort of like this. She just couldn't concentrate on both at the same time. It was moving too fast.

Then Maxine confessed to certain things she had once done at summer camp. Last year with a boy named Ernie Gilhooley, when they were both in sick bay with a summer flu. "Ew, you both had the flu?" said Laura. "And you did *that*?"

"We couldn't get infected, we already were," said Maxine, with hapless logic. "How about you, Laura? Have you ever slept with a boy?"

Well. It came down to that. Had Laura ever slept with a boy? Was he a boy? Was he a swan? It had been too hard to tell at the time, and it was too hard to tell now, so Laura had said the only thing possible. It was true both in her imagination and in dark of night. "I'm not telling," she said.

The Delaware and Hudson train racked and rattled

along the river. The cabin smelled of chicken lo mein and Lysol. A few of the travelers seemed to have had some early drinks in the Oyster Bar at Grand Central Station; it was New Year's Eve after all. Laura looked at the postcard she had picked up. The Manhattan skyline at night, golden jeweled lights stacked in buildings profiled against blackness. She turned the card over. She had already addressed the card to Sam Roscoe. The message area was still blank, though.

She took the pen she'd filched from Nonno's desk. It said CIARDI'S FINE FOODS AND DELICACIES on it in sober capitals. To this pen she had attached a single white swan feather she'd found in a fold of her bedspread when she woke on Christmas morning. She'd wrapped a rubber band around the pen's pocket clip and the hollow quill of the stem. It was a pen, it was a bayonet, it was a signal. Tightening her hand around it, she was able to write.

Dear Sam someday I'd like to see where you let Fluster go free into the wild. Would you show me, from your friend Laura C.

It was a beginning but it seemed complete in itself, enough for her to feel satisfied.

Then she took the envelope that her ticket had been

stored in and scribbled on the back. Her words looked foreign but the sound of them was intimate somehow. She had heard words in her head for such a long time. She would keep trying to tell herself into her own life.

Someday I will learn to write. Someday, maybe, I will learn to write. Someday I may be able to write the truth.

The white-whiskered conductor came through. "Next stop Hudson, Albany after that," he croaked to everyone. He sounded as if he had nodules on his vocal cords—a cold, or maybe cancer. Because Mary Bernice had asked him to give Laura special attention, he singled her out as he passed her seat. "Understand, Miss? Don't get off this stop. I'll help you with your luggage when the time comes. About forty-five minutes give or take."

Though alone, she leaned against the glass, feeling well taken care of. The Hudson River Valley looked vaguely like Japan because it was snowing yet again, and everything was black and white. Black water, white ice, white air, black trees. An old lady on the platform at Hudson struggled with a man's umbrella against the clotting snow. Laura tucked the postcard into her handbag and began to tidy her belongings. Albany next stop.

She straightened the collar of her good Macy's coat. Nonna di Lorenzo and that mysterious Umberto were going to meet Laura's train at Albany Union Station. They would drive Laura out to the Ann Lee nursing home in the countryside. Laura would go into her mother's room and, whether she was still alert or whether it was too late, Laura would sit down on the bed next to her. Maybe even lie down on the bed. And then Laura would spread over her mother whatever harboring wing she had in herself to spread.

"Ready to go, young lady?" asked the conductor.

"Guess so."

"That's the ticket, buttercup." Despite Laura's protest, he took her suitcase for her. He hummed while bumping it down the aisle. "Repeat the sounding joy, repeat the sounding joy, repeat, repeat the sounding joy," he warbled, mostly to himself. "Christmas is over a week already but the song, well, it repeats the sounding joy. Can't shake it."

Standing in the corridor, she leaned down to look out the windows. Across the southbound tracks, across the badlands of snowy bracken and abandoned tires and pools of Hudson River backwater, she could see the broad ribbon of river. Black as a tarred road. Then, as she watched, out on the open water a single swan swept up from some hidden cranny. It paced itself in the snowy air more or less across from her window. Moving at the same rate, but out in the wild. Heading north. It was single, yes—unless you counted its reflection, which made it a pair of swans.

Acknowledgments

Many thanks to a few friends whose support has been as welcome as it has been kind. In no particular order, my gratitude is due to my husband, Andy Newman, and to Maggie Terris for close readings of an early draft; to Zach and Ana Tarpagos who, one rainy night in Athens, selected and played flute duets on the subject of swans at a reading in the home of Nikos Trivoulidis and Christos Lygas; to Barbara Harrison and the Examined Life team for inviting me again to Greece where I introduced this story to that convivial assembly; to concert singer Anne Azéma, who supplied me the Carolingian lyric and her translation that launches this story; to Stephen Guerriero for his recollections of Guerriero family Christmas Eve feasts of the seven fishes; to Cassie Jones and her team at Harper-Collins, of course; to Scott McKowen for his evocative cover artwork; and to P. L. Travers, in loving memory, whose remark to me, about a year before she died, may have been the initial prompt for this novel.